BERGMAN MANOR

by

Tara J. Stone

FADE IN:

EXT. BERGMAN MANOR - GARDEN - NIGHT (1925)

Moonlight filters through a swirling mist to bathe a well
kept garden in an eerie glow. Towering over the garden is
a huge mansion -- Bergman Manor.

All is quiet except for WAVES CRASHING against a cliff
somewhere nearby.

Until a DOOR SLAMS.

GRAVEL CRUNCHES under RUNNING FEET.

The RUNNER, a young man in a dinner jacket, glances over
his shoulder and slips on the gravel as he turns a corner
around a hedge of bushes.

He ducks behind a bush and tries to calm his breathing
long enough to listen.

There's nothing for a beat or two. And then...

SLOW, MEASURED FOOTSTEPS on the GRAVEL. Coming CLOSER.

The Runner braces himself, takes a breath, and sprints.

OVER BLACK

A BLOOD-CURDLING SCREAM. Impossible to tell if it comes
from a man or a woman.

                                        CUT TO:

INT. BERGMAN MANOR - DOROTHY'S ROOM - SAME

A pretty young woman no more than 20, DOROTHY FRANCIS,
sits up in bed as if waking from a nightmare.

There's a BONE-CRACKING THUD, THUD, THUD...

                    DOROTHY
          No. Not again.

Dorothy covers her ears, and when that doesn't seem to
work, she hides her face under her pillow.

EXT. BERGMAN MANOR - CLIFF - NIGHT

Clouds obscure the moonlight.

The Runner's face seems to float over the ground. He's being dragged.

FROM BELOW

A body tumbles over the edge and hurtles TOWARD CAMERA.

                                        CUT TO BLACK.

FADE IN:

CLOSE UP

Wide, staring eyes. They look lifeless... until they blink.

EXT. PARK BENCH - MORNING

The eyes belong to CLEM BEAUREGARD, a disheveled but handsome fella in his early 20s. He's sprawled on a park bench, just waking up.

He sits up slowly and puts a hand to his aching head. He looks around, trying to figure out where he is and how he got there.

He does a quick pat of all his pockets and feels something in the inside pocket of his jacket. He pulls it out: it's a champagne cork.

He remembers and smiles.

He picks a flower from a bush nearby.

INT. OFFICE - MORNING

The words on the glass door read:

"J. ALAN MONTGOMERY

PRIVATE INVESTIGATOR"

Clem comes in silently and hangs his hat on the rack. He still doesn't look quite put together.

The secretary, JANE MILLER (20s), has her back to the door, leaning over a filing cabinet.

Clem sneaks up behind her and gives her a peck on the cheek. When she turns in shock, he holds up the flower from the park. She rolls her eyes, but she's not angry -- this is a game they've played before.

                    JANE
          The answer is still no.

                    CLEM
          How come?

She buttons Clem's top shirt button and tightens his tie. Then she takes the flower from him and sticks it in a small vase full of several other flowers in various states of wilted-ness.

                    JANE
          Because I only date men. Not boys.

Clem glances toward the door leading to the inner office.

                    CLEM
          Is he in?

                    JANE
          And furious.

                    CLEM
          Because I'm late?

                    JANE
          Because he knows why.

                    CLEM
          Wish me luck.

                    JANE
          You'll need more than that.

Clem goes through a door and into...

INT. MONTGOMERY'S OFFICE - SAME

PAPERS SHUFFLE across the floor when Clem opens the door.

MONTY, an intense-looking man in his 30s, stands in the middle of a room littered with newspapers. He flips through a paper yellow with age. Half of the middle finger on his right hand is missing.

Clem treads carefully, trying to avoid stepping on a potentially important article, but it's impossible.

                    MONTY
          Where have you been? Never mind,
          don't answer that. I don't want to
          know.

                    CLEM
          What's all this?

He motions to all the papers strewn around the room.

                    MONTY
          A case.

Clem waits for Monty to explain further, but he doesn't.

                    CLEM
          What are you looking for?

Monty throws aside the paper he has and walks around the room looking at the dates on the papers on the floor.

                    MONTY
          Summer, 1923.

Clem looks around for any corresponding dates.

                    CLEM
          What happened in the summer of
          1923?

                    MONTY
          Aha!

He picks up a paper and flips through it. He finds what he's looking for and becomes engrossed.

Clem waits.

                    MONTY (CONT'D)
          That makes...
               (counting on his
                fingers)
          Four in the last five years.

                    CLEM
          Four what?

Suddenly Monty looks up.

                    MONTY
          Clem, you're fired.

                         CLEM
            What?

                         MONTY
            I've gone too easy on you for too
            long. Look at you, you can't even
            get your buttons right.

Clem looks down at his vest, and indeed, the buttons are
off by one hole. He goes about fixing them.

                         MONTY (CONT'D)
            Give me one good reason I should
            keep paying you to come in late
            every morning and do nothing.

                         CLEM
            I'll do better, Uncle Monty.
            Honest. If you'd just let me join
            you on a case --

Monty snorts.

                         MONTY
            This job takes brains, Clem. And
            hard work. Not exactly your strong
            suits.

                         CLEM
            That's hardly fair. In five years
            the closest I've come to a case is
            organizing the paperwork after
            it's been solved. You've never
            even given me a chance.

                         MONTY
            To do what? Uncover information
            that has the power to destroy or
            save lives? You think I should
            hand that kind of responsibility
            over to a dewdropper like you?

Monty gathers up several papers that he's organized into
one neat pile in the midst of the surrounding chaos.

                         CLEM
            So that's it. No warning or
            anything. I'm just... fired.

Monty looks at Clem and sighs.

                          MONTY
           I'll give you one more shot, but
           only because your sainted mother
           made me promise to look after you.
           I'll be gone for several days. If
           you can manage to show up to work
           on time every day and hold down
           the fort until I get back, you can
           join me on my next case. If Jane
           tells me you've been late even
           once... you're fired. Got it?

Clem nods. Monty waves a hand at the mess of newspapers.

                          MONTY (CONT'D)
           You can start by cleaning this up.

And he's gone.

Clem stands in the middle of the trashed room,
bewildered. Finally, he bends to gather up the papers.

INT. OFFICE - MORNING

When Clem emerges from the inner office, Monty is gone.
Jane looks up expectantly.

                          CLEM
           He almost fired me.

                          JANE
           I know.

                          CLEM
           Sometimes I think he's sorry he
           ever took me in.

                          JANE
           That can't be true.

                          CLEM
           Sure seems that way.

                          JANE
           Well, things aren't always what
           they seem.

EXT. JAZZ CLUB - EVENING

Clem strolls down the sidewalk of a busy downtown street,
hands in his pockets. A couple comes out of an unassuming
door, and JAZZ MUSIC floats out behind them.

Clem stops and looks at the door. He turns to keep walking, but he can't resist. He goes inside.

EXT. STREET - EARLY MORNING

Clem stumbles out of another club door with his arm around a GIRL. They laugh drunkenly. Clem blinks at the morning light. He checks his watch and sobers.

> CLEM
> Oh, gee. I gotta get to work.

> GIRL
> Aw, come on. We could go to my
> place. My roommate's out of town.

She leans in for a kiss, but Clem uses every ounce of willpower to resist.

> CLEM
> I can't. I'm sorry. I'll call you
> later.

He trots toward a taxi on the corner, leaving the Girl standing on the sidewalk with her hands on her hips.

INT. OFFICE - MORNING

Clem flies through the door. Jane looks up from the desk and looks at the clock on the wall.

> JANE
> Just made it.

Clem breathes a sigh of relief.

> JANE (CONT'D)
> Tomorrow you should try a fresh
> set of clothes though.

Clem looks down at his rumpled suit, chastened.

INT. APARTMENT BUILDING - HALLWAY - AFTERNOON

Clem approaches his door. He inserts his latchkey, but it doesn't work. He tries again, and jiggles the handle.

Suddenly, the door flies open, and a large MAN in an UNDERSHIRT opens the door.

                    UNDERSHIRT MAN
          What the hell is going on out
          here?

                         CLEM
          Who are you? What are you doing in
          my apartment?

                    UNDERSHIRT MAN
          Oh, so you're the bum who used to
          live here.

He reaches behind the door and produces a large sack. He
shoves it into Clem's hands.

                    UNDERSHIRT MAN (CONT'D)
          Your things.

He's about to shut the door, but Clem slaps a hand on the
door to keep it open.

                         CLEM
          Wait, what is this?

                    UNDERSHIRT MAN
          Guess you shoulda been better
          'bout paying your rent. You got a
          problem, talk to the landlord.

He SLAMS the DOOR shut. Clem is stunned.

EXT. APARTMENT BUILDING - MOMENTS LATER

Clem comes out of the building, clutching his sack of
belongings to his chest. A HOBO sits just feet away from
the door.

                         HOBO
          Hey, pal. Can you spare some
          change?

Clem looks around at the Hobo. He digs into a pocket and
pulls out a handful of coins. He starts to count it out,
but he looks back at the Hobo and gives him the whole
handful.

                       HOBO (CONT'D)
          Thanks, buddy. You look like you
          could use a drink.

The Hobo holds up a paper sack.

Clem seriously considers it for a moment, but finally shakes his head and walks away.

EXT. PARK BENCH - EVENING

Clem sits on the park bench, his sack leaning nearby.

He watches a happy couple walking arm-in-arm.

A soft wind blows, and Clem pulls up his collar and wraps his jacket more tightly around him.

A rowdy group of FLAPPER GIRLS and their handsome fellas on their way to a nightclub or a party approaches. Clem tries to hide his face from them, but it's too late.

                    FLAPPER GIRL
          Clem Beauregard, is that you?

Clem comes out from behind his jacket collar.

                    CLEM
          Hiya!

                    FLAPPER GIRL
          Hey, we're on our way to Quincy's
          new club. Want to join?

                    CLEM
          No, really. I shouldn't tonight.

                    FLAPPER GIRL
          All right. Well, enjoy your bench!

They all laugh and move on.

Clem rubs his hands together to warm them. He sticks them in his pockets and discovers something there. He pulls out a key.

INT. OFFICE - NIGHT

Light from the hallway filters through the glass door, making a shadow of Monty's name across the floor.

A silhouette appears outside the door. Inserts a key in the door. The door swings open.

INT. MONTGOMERY'S OFFICE - NIGHT

The light flickers on. Clem stands in the doorway with
his sack of stuff.

He eyes the sofa against the wall opposite the desk.

He sighs.

INT. OFFICE - MORNING

Jane unlocks the door and enters. She takes off her hat
and settles into the seat at her desk.

She rifles through the papers on her desk, grabs a
couple, and walks to the door leading to Monty's office.

INT. MONTGOMERY'S OFFICE - SAME

Jane opens the door and turns on the light... and
screams!

Clem flies off the sofa. He's wearing pajamas.

                    CLEM
          What? What happened?

                    JANE
          Clem, you scared the daylights out
          of me! What are you doing here?

                    CLEM
          Never mind that. I'm here on time,
          right?

                    JANE
          You're not telling me you stayed
          here all night just to be
          punctual. Anyway, I don't think it
          really counts if you're not
          dressed.

                    CLEM
          Okay, you win. My landlord kicked
          me out.

                    JANE
          Well, you can't stay here. If
          Monty finds out...

                    CLEM
        I know, I know. I just need time
        to find a new place, that's all.

A voice floats in from the reception area.

                    VOICE (O.S.)
        Hello?

INT. OFFICE - SAME

A sweaty, middle-aged man in a brown suit, DETECTIVE
GATES, stands before the desk. Jane comes from the inner
office and shuts the door behind her. Detective Gates
eyes her salaciously.

                    JANE
        Good morning, sir. May I help you?

Detective Gates looks back at the name on the door.

                    DETECTIVE GATES
        You Mr. Montgomery's secretary?

                    JANE
        Yes, sir.

                    DETECTIVE GATES
        Name's Gates. Detective Gates.

He produces a badge.

                    DETECTIVE GATES (CONT'D)
        Can you tell me who Mr.
        Montgomery's next-of-kin is?

                    JANE
        Why? Has something happened?

                    DETECTIVE GATES
        If you'll just answer my question,
        please.

                    JANE
        I suppose it would be his nephew,
        Clem. Clement Beauregard.

                    DETECTIVE GATES
        Can you tell me how to get in
        touch with Mr. Beauregard?

> JANE
> As a matter of fact, he's here.
> Just one moment, please.

She's clearly unsettled, but she picks up the phone.

> JANE (CONT'D)
> Clem, there's a Detective Gates
> here. He wants to see Mr.
> Montgomery's next-of-kin. Are you
> dress-- are you able to see
> Detective Gates?

Detective Gates catches the slip and gives her a knowing
look. She sets the phone down.

> JANE (CONT'D)
> Go right in, Detective.

Detective Gates walks through the door leading to the
inner office.

INT. MONTGOMERY'S OFFICE - SAME

Clem finishes buttoning his shirt as Detective Gates
enters.

Detective Gates glances back toward Jane's desk and gives
Clem a look almost like admiration.

Clem offers a hand, and Detective Gates takes it.

> CLEM
> What can I do for you, Detective?

> DETECTIVE GATES
> Clement Beauregard? You work here?

> CLEM
> Yes. And please, call me Clem.

> DETECTIVE GATES
> You're Mr. Montgomery's nephew?

> CLEM
> That's right. He's my uncle. My
> mother's younger brother.
> (off Gates' look)
> Much younger.

Gates helps himself to the seat in front of Montgomery's
desk and motions for Clem to sit as well.

                    CLEM (CONT'D)
          What's this all about, Detective?

                    DETECTIVE GATES
          Forgive me. I suppose I should
          have started with a proper
          introduction. I'm with the Lincoln
          County Sheriff's Department.

He produces his badge again.

                    CLEM
          Lincoln County? What brings you
          all the way down here?

                    DETECTIVE GATES
          The worst part of my job, Mr.
          Beauregard. I'm here to inform you
          that Mr. Montgomery is dead.

Clem is shocked.

                    DETECTIVE GATES (CONT'D)
          Am I to understand you had no
          knowledge of Mr. Montgomery's
          whereabouts?

                    CLEM
          No. What happened?

                    DETECTIVE GATES
          Did Mr. Montgomery ever mention a
          place called Bergman Manor?

                    CLEM
          I don't think so.

                    DETECTIVE GATES
          Are you aware of any cases Mr.
          Montgomery might have been working
          on that would have taken him to
          Bergman Manor?

                    CLEM
          No. He told me he would be gone
          for several days, but he didn't
          tell me where he was going or why.

                    DETECTIVE GATES
          Would the secretary know?

Clem picks up his phone.

                         CLEM
              Jane, could you come in here,
              please?

He sets down the phone, and Jane appears within seconds.

                         JANE
              Yes, sir?

                         CLEM
              Jane, Monty's dead.

Jane covers her mouth.

                         DETECTIVE GATES
              Do you know what he was working on
              at Bergman Manor?

Jane looks from Clem to Detective Gates and takes her
time answering.

                         JANE
              No. I'm sorry, I don't.

Detective Gates doesn't know if he should believe her.

                         DETECTIVE GATES
              Uh-huh. Well, that's all the
              confirmation I need.

                         CLEM
              Confirmation of what?

                         DETECTIVE GATES
              Self-inflicted.

                         CLEM
              Suicide?

                         DETECTIVE GATES
              Maybe. Maybe an accident. Mr.
              Montgomery drowned in the ocean.

                         CLEM
              How can you be sure no one else
              forced him to drown? Were there
              any witnesses?

                         MR. GATES
              No, but everyone else at the Manor
              had an alibi. No one there
              acknowledged any connection to
              him. Most didn't even know his
              name.
                         (MORE)

                              MR. GATES (CONT'D)
                    So if you say he wasn't working a
                    case there... What other
                    conclusion can I draw?

INT. OFFICE - MOMENTS LATER

The door to the inner office opens and Gates walks
through. Jane and Clem follow shortly. When Gates is
safely out the door:

                              CLEM
                    Jane, why did you lie?

Jane looks surprised.

                              CLEM (CONT'D)
                    You know as well as I do he was
                    working a case at Bergman Manor.

                              JANE
                    Yes. But...

                              CLEM
                    But what?

                              JANE
                    It's ridiculous. At least I
                    thought it was. Now I'm not so
                    sure.

                              CLEM
                    What was he working on?

                              JANE
                    Bergman Manor is... it's supposed
                    to be haunted or some such thing.

                              CLEM
                    Monty wasn't that gullible.

                              JANE
                    I don't know, Clem. When the case
                    came in, I thought the same thing,
                    but he was like a man possessed.
                    I've never seen him so excited
                    about a case.

                              CLEM
                    So... what? You lied because you
                    didn't want to tell Detective
                    Gates that you suspect Monty's
                    murderer might be a ghost?

Jane shrugs helplessly.

                    CLEM (CONT'D)
          Well, it is ridiculous.

                    JANE
          And yet, Monty is dead.

                    CLEM
          You said when the case came in.
          Who brought him the case? Who
          hired him?

                    JANE
          That's another strange thing. I
          don't think anyone hired him.

                    CLEM
          Then what made him want to go
          there? What was he investigating?

Jane shrugs again.

INT. MONTGOMERY'S OFFICE - DAY

Newspapers litter the room again. Clem stands in the
middle of the room sans jacket and tie, vest and shirt
collar unbuttoned, sleeves rolled up, reading a newspaper
clipping.

Jane comes in with another stack of papers.

                    JANE
          I found more at the library on 5th
          and Main. Any clues yet?

                    CLEM
          How far back do those go?

                    JANE
          The oldest goes back about twenty
          years.

                    CLEM
          Look at this.

Clem gathers a couple other clippings and shows them all
to Jane.

                              CLEM (CONT'D)
          In the last five years, four
          guests of Bergman Manor have died,
          five including Monty. All apparent
          accidents or suicides.

                              JANE
          Remind me never to vacation there.

                              CLEM
          You're safe. They were all men.

                              JANE
          Bad luck.

                              CLEM
          What was Monty's first rule of
          good investigating?

                              JANE
          Husbands who work late are always
          cheating.

                              CLEM
          Right. There are no coincidences.

                              JANE
          You think they were all murdered?

                              CLEM
          Give me the old one, from twenty
          years ago.

Jane hands it to him, and he flips through to an article
on Bergman Manor. Jane gets distracted by an
advertisement sitting on the desk: "Experience the
THRILLS and CHILLS of a night at HAUNTED Bergman Manor."

                              CLEM (CONT'D)
          Ah, here we are. "Mistress Of
          Bergman Manor Jumps Off Cliff,
          Commits Suicide."

Jane holds up the strange advertisement.

                              JANE
          Could she be the ghost of Bergman
          Manor?

Clem gives her an irritated look.

                              JANE (CONT'D)
          What? You said there were no
          coincidences.
                              (MORE)

> JANE (CONT'D)
> Maybe she's the one who's been
> killing all these gentlemen.
> They're descendants of all the
> lovers who scorned her. Or thieves
> she caught stealing the family
> silver.

> CLEM
> And which one of those was Uncle
> Monty supposed to be?

Jane concedes with a shrug.

> CLEM (CONT'D)
> Monty was clearly interested in
> these men's deaths, but why? And
> what did he have in common with
> them that made him the murderer's
> next victim?

> JANE
> You didn't find anything in his
> things?

Clem nods to the advertisement in Jane's hand.

> CLEM
> Just that ad, and this old
> photograph.

He reaches around Jane to grab a photograph from the
desk. He holds it up for her.

It's old, turn-of-the-century. An elderly woman with a
parasol stands with a boy of 12 in front of a hedge of
well-trimmed bushes. The boy is missing part of the
middle finger on his right hand.

EXT. BERGMAN MANOR - DAY

Bergman Manor overlooks a steep seaside cliff. The
grounds are well kept. It might be beautiful in broad
daylight, but a heavy rain makes the whole thing gloomy
and a little unsettling.

A heavily cloaked figure runs from the ten-car garage,
across the lawn and the gravel drive toward the house.

In a window on an upper floor, the dim outline of
somebody watches the running figure.

INT. BERGMAN MANOR - DINING HALL - SAME

Inside, the atmosphere is warm and inviting. Several
patrons sit around a long, communal table and chat
amiably.

At the head of the table sits a distinguished looking
gentleman in his 50s -- HORACE COOPER.

To his right, two attractive women in their 40s who must
be sisters -- IRMA and EILEEN PRICE -- are enthralled by
whatever Horace says.

To his left, a couple also listens to Horace and ignores
their two young boys, who are shoving and hitting each
other -- the TOBIN family.

At the other end of the table sits a man in his 60s --
DR. CAMPBELL.

An old but elegant French woman -- MADAME GUILLAUME --
chats away at Dr. Campbell, though it's anyone's guess
whether he's listening. Next to her sits a bored young
woman of 18, her granddaughter -- MARIE GUILLAUME.

A young couple, clearly newlyweds, rounds out the group --
SAMUEL and LILLIAN SELMER.

From somewhere, a DOOR OPENS and SLAMS SHUT. A moment
later, the cloaked figure from outside appears. As the
soaking figure hurries through the room and sheds a heavy
overcoat, we see that it's Dorothy. She disappears
through a swinging door into...

INT. BERGMAN MANOR - KITCHEN - SAME

Dorothy barely makes it through the door before a strong
hand grabs her and whips her around. She stands toe-to-
toe with a giant of a man in his 40s. This is ODIN
BERGMAN.

                    ODIN
          Where have you been? The guests
          have been waiting.

MRS. O'TOOLE, the cook, pretends not to notice the
confrontation.

Dorothy jerks her arm free of Odin's grasp.

                    DOROTHY
          I'm here now.

                         ODIN
          You're pushing your luck, Dorothy.

                       DOROTHY
          What are you going to do, Mr.
          Bergman? Fire me?

She throws her dripping coat on a rack, grabs a tray
loaded with food, and heads back to the dining hall.

INT. BERGMAN MANOR - DINING HALL - SAME

As Dorothy serves the food to the patrons around the
table, the front DOOR OPENS and SHUTS again.

A moment later, a handsome man in his 20s, THOMAS COOPER,
comes in and takes a seat next to Eileen. Marie's gaze
follows him, but Thomas's eyes are trained on Dorothy.

Although a smile flickers across Dorothy's lips, she
avoids making eye contact with Thomas.

A PHONE RINGS in another room.

INT. BERGMAN MANOR - ODIN'S OFFICE - DAY

Odin is on the telephone when Dorothy enters with a plate
of food for him.

                         ODIN
                  (into the phone)
          Yes, it was terrible. Yes. Well,
          thank you for everything,
          Detective.

Dorothy sets the food on the desk in front of Odin as he
hangs up the phone.

                       DOROTHY
          The police?

                         ODIN
          They've finished their
          investigation. Poor devil.

                       DOROTHY
          Was he... did he...

                         ODIN
          Whatever happened, he did it to
          himself.

Dorothy doesn't respond, but she doesn't seem convinced.

                    DOROTHY
          That's two this summer.

Odin looks up from his food.

                    DOROTHY (CONT'D)
          You don't think --

                    ODIN
          No. I don't.

Dorothy stands deep in thought for several moments. Odin
watches her.

                    ODIN (CONT'D)
          Dorothy.

Dorothy snaps out of her reverie. He looks and nods
toward the door to get her going again.

                    DOROTHY
          Of course. Excuse me.

She hurries from the room.

INT. BERGMAN MANOR - DINING HALL - LATER

Dorothy works her way around the table clearing dishes.

                    HORACE
          Thomas, my boy. Before you
          arrived, I was telling our dear
          friends here about Eleanor.

                    EILEEN
          Yes, your father tells us you are
          to be married at the end of the
          summer.

Dorothy drops a dish in front of Horace, spilling all
over him. Horace jumps up.

                    HORACE
          Damn it, girl!

                    DOROTHY
          I'm so sorry, Mr. Cooper.

Dorothy sets her load of dirty dishes on a side table and
hurries to offer a napkin. Horace rips it from her hand.

                    HORACE
          Do you know how much this suit
          cost me? And look what you've
          done, you stupid thing.

                    THOMAS
          Father.

                    DR. CAMPBELL
          Really, Horace. You're frightening
          the poor girl. She didn't do it on
          purpose.

Embarrassed and angry, Dorothy runs out of the room.

INT. BERGMAN MANOR - SERVANTS' QUARTERS - LATER

Thomas tiptoes down the hallway with an eye over his
shoulder. He nearly bumps into Dorothy coming out of her
room.

                    THOMAS
          Dorothy --

                    DOROTHY
          Excuse me, sir, I have duties to
          attend to.

She tries to pass him, but he steps in front of her.

                    THOMAS
          Please, Dorothy. I want to
          explain.

                    DOROTHY
          I don't know what else you could
          possibly explain. You are engaged
          to be married. I may be a simple
          servant, but I do understand that.

                    THOMAS
          You don't understand at all. It
          was a foolish childhood promise
          that I thought we both understood
          was in jest. But she didn't see it
          that way, and more importantly,
          neither did our fathers.

                    DOROTHY
          If I had known I never would've --

                         THOMAS
               I know, and it was unfair of me
               not to tell you.

He brushes his knuckles across her cheek.

                         THOMAS (CONT'D)
               Forgive me?

He leans in to kiss her.

                         ODIN (O.S.)
               Dorothy.

Thomas and Dorothy jump at Odin's voice. He stands at the
end of the hallway behind Thomas.

                         ODIN (CONT'D)
               Mrs. O'Toole needs you in the
               kitchen.

Dorothy starts past Thomas, but he stops her and
whispers:

                         THOMAS
               Meet me in the gazebo later?

Dorothy doesn't respond. She shrugs off his grip and
hurries past Odin, disappearing around the corner.

Thomas half smiles at Odin, but Odin is not pleased.

INT. BERGMAN MANOR - LIBRARY - EVENING

Odin stands at the window, peering out through the
drapes. Irma and Eileen sit near him, chattering away.

                         IRMA
               Well, I still say I saw something
               that night.

Odin scowls at what he sees outside.

ODIN'S POV - THROUGH WINDOW

Dorothy meets Thomas under the gazebo. The rain has
mostly stopped by now.

                         EILEEN (V.O.)
              Of course you did. But are you
              sure it was the ghost of Bergman
              Manor, or was it the whole bottle
              of gin you'd put away that night?
              It was quite a brawl, remember.

                         IRMA (V.O.)
              Hush, Eileen. What will Mr.
              Bergman think of us?

                         EILEEN (V.O.)
              As if he doesn't already know.

Thomas tries to kiss Dorothy, but she pulls away. He
becomes more insistent and presses his mouth to hers.

BACK TO SCENE

Dr. Campbell joins Odin at the window and follows his
gaze.

                         DR. CAMPBELL
              Not very discreet, are they?

Odin lets the drapes drop.

                         ODIN
              Fools. Both of them.

EXT. BERGMAN MANOR - GAZEBO - SAME

Dorothy pulls away from Thomas and slaps him. She stalks
away as he rubs his stinging cheek.

INT. BERGMAN MANOR - THOMAS'S ROOM - NIGHT

Thomas enters and shuts the door. As he undoes his tie,
he notices something on the bed.

A note scrawled in unsettling script.

"STAY AWAY FROM HER"

Thomas looks around as if he might catch the note's
author still in his room. Looking at the note again, he
crumples it and tosses it aside. It tumbles beneath the
bed.

INT. MONTGOMERY'S OFFICE - NIGHT

Jane sleeps on the sofa opposite Montgomery's desk. Clem
sits behind the desk and examines the old photograph. He
tosses the photo on the desk and rubs his eyes.

He stands and walks to Jane. Crouching beside her, he
gently strokes her arm.

                    CLEM
          Jane, darling.

Jane's eyes flutter open. She sits up, and Clem sits next
to her.

                    JANE
          What did you find?

                    CLEM
          Nothing. I don't think I will find
          anything here.

                    JANE
          You're giving up?

                    CLEM
          I hate to ask, Jane, but... I need
          to borrow some money. Just enough
          to get me to Bergman Manor.

Jane raises her eyebrows.

EXT. BERGMAN MANOR - AFTERNOON

The rain has returned with force. A car drops off a
passenger at the front door.

INT. BERGMAN MANOR - FOYER - SAME

As Dorothy hurries up the stairs, the front door opens,
and in steps Clem.

                    CLEM
          Excuse me.

But Dorothy doesn't hear him. She disappears at the top
of the stairs.

Clem sets down his suitcase and removes his hat. He takes
in his surroundings.

To his left, the DIN of the GUESTS in the dining room floats through the open door. To his right, another open door leads to what must be a library.

Someone or something flashes across the library doorway.

                    CLEM (CONT'D)
          Hello?

He starts toward the library.

INT. BERGMAN MANOR - LIBRARY - SAME

Clem steps through the doorway.

The room is empty.

Across from the doorway is a huge fireplace, and above the mantle hangs a giant portrait of a beautiful young woman. Something about the woman in the portrait resembles Dorothy, but it's clearly not her.

Clem walks across the room, studying the picture.

                    ODIN (O.S.)
          May I help you?

Clem turns at the sound. Odin stands in the doorway.

                    CLEM
          Beautiful woman.

                    ODIN
          You must belong to the wet
          suitcase out in the hall.

                    CLEM
          Yes, my secretary called ahead to
          make a reservation for me.
          Beauregard's the name.

                    ODIN
          Ah, yes. You're lucky. Got the
          last room. I'm Odin Bergman.
          Welcome to my humble
          establishment.

Odin offers a hand, which Clem shakes warmly.

INT. BERGMAN MANOR - CLEM'S ROOM - LATER

Odin opens the door for Clem and sets his suitcase down just inside.

                    CLEM
          Thank you.

                    ODIN
          Ring if you need anything. Lunch
          has just been served and supper is
          at six-thirty.

Odin leaves, shutting the door behind him.

Clem sets his suitcase on the bed and begins to unpack.

INT. BERGMAN MANOR - THOMAS'S ROOM - SAME

Dorothy makes the bed.

Thomas enters behind her and watches her with a smile for a moment.

                    THOMAS
          You make it awfully hard for a
          fella to get over you.

Dorothy turns, startled.

                    THOMAS (CONT'D)
          You know, I didn't say anything to
          Mr. Bergman about your behavior
          last night, but I could. How do
          you think he would react if he
          learned that the maid attacked a
          guest?

                    DOROTHY
          Excuse me, sir.

She moves toward the door, but Thomas stands in the doorway.

For a tense moment, it's a silent standoff. Finally, Thomas steps aside, and Dorothy leaves.

INT. BERGMAN MANOR - HALLWAY - SAME

Dorothy hurries toward the stairs and nearly bowls over Clem, coming out of his room, as she passes him. He grabs her wrist, stopping her.

                         CLEM
               Always in a hurry.

He's charming, not mean. But Dorothy's in no mood for it.

                         DOROTHY
               Yes, sir. Is there something you
               wanted, sir?

                         CLEM
               Your name, perhaps?

Dorothy looks past Clem and sees Thomas emerging from his
room.

                         DOROTHY
               Excuse me, sir.

She pulls away from him and continues on her way.

INT. BERGMAN MANOR - DINING HALL - MOMENTS LATER

Clem enters the room. Most of the other guests are
already seated and finishing their meal. Only Thomas and
the Guillaumes are missing.

Clem goes to the side board to dish up.

Irma spots Clem.

                         IRMA
               Ooh, a new victim!

                         EILEEN
               Oh, how delightful! You must sit
               next to us. We're the life of the
               party.

Clem smiles and takes a seat between the Price sisters.

                         CLEM
               And just whose victim am I
               agreeing to become?

                         IRMA
               Irma and Eileen Price, and I
               promise we'll make it as painless
               as possible.

                         CLEM
               Clem Beauregard, and I look
               forward to it.

The Price sisters giggle.

Horace offers a hand.

> HORACE
> Horace Cooper. Glad to have you
> with us, Mr. Beauregard.

> CLEM
> Please, call me Clem.

> HORACE
> These are the Tobins. Arthur and
> Nora, and their boys, Timothy and
> Walter.

The Tobins smile and nod.

> EILEEN
> And down there are Samuel and
> Lillian Selmer, just married. And
> next to them is Dr. Campbell. Hard
> of hearing, keeps mostly to
> himself. One of Mr. Bergman's
> oldest friends.

Thomas enters.

> IRMA
> Ah, and this is Horace's son,
> Thomas.

Thomas takes a seat next to Irma.

> IRMA (CONT'D)
> Thomas, this is Clem. He's come to
> spice up our party.

> THOMAS
> Your timing is impeccable. With
> this dreary weather, we were all
> starting to get bored, I think.

> CLEM
> I can't do anything about the
> weather, but I'll do my best to
> make things a little more
> interesting.

Madame and Marie Guillaume enter and take their seats.
Marie smiles coyly at Thomas, and he winks at her.

                    EILEEN
              (in a low voice)
        Madame Guillaume and her
        granddaughter, Marie. I'm not sure
        the girl speaks any English, and
        what the old bag says you can't
        understand anyway. A perfect match
        for Dr. Campbell, really.

She giggles at her own joke, and Clem smiles politely.

Dorothy enters with fresh coffee.

Clem leans toward Eileen and matches her secretive tone.

                    CLEM
        And what about her?

                    EILEEN
        Who, the maid? Why on Earth would
        you want to know about her?

Horace joins the conversation, but speaks loudly enough
for Dorothy to hear.

                    HORACE
        A clumsy and insolent creature.
        Dumped food all over me yesterday.

Dorothy hears it but pretends not to. Clem watches her
with great interest.

Eileen brings the volume of the conversation back down.

                    EILEEN
        They say Mr. Bergman found her on
        his doorstep when she was just a
        child and took pity on the poor
        thing. He gave the girl a place to
        live and little jobs to do around
        the Manor. Eventually worked her
        way up to being Bergman's right
        hand man, if you'll excuse the
        expression. She's practically a
        fixture now.

Eileen cuts off her speech as Dorothy nears.

                    CLEM
        What's her name?

                    DOROTHY
        Dorothy Francis.

Dorothy pours coffee for Thomas, but her words are aimed at Clem.

                    DOROTHY (CONT'D)
          If you wish to know about me, sir,
          you might ask me yourself rather
          than listening to rumors from idle
          tongues.

                    CLEM
          Perhaps I would, but you always
          seem to be in such a hurry.

Dorothy pours Clem a cup of coffee and leaves.

                    HORACE
          What did I tell you. Insolent. If
          Bergman isn't careful, such an ill-
          mannered servant will scare away
          all his business.

                    CLEM
          Ah! The truth comes out about
          who's been haunting Bergman Manor.

Some people chuckle, but:

                    IRMA
          Oh no. Make no mistake. This place
          is haunted.

                    NORA
          I wish you wouldn't talk about
          such things in front of the
          children. You frighten them.

                    IRMA
          All the same, it is haunted.
          Eileen and I have often heard
          strange things at night, haven't
          we, Eileen?

                    EILEEN
          Oh yes. And haven't any of you had
          the feeling you see something or
          someone out of the corner of your
          eye, but as soon as you look...
          nothing?

                    TIMOTHY
          I have!

                    WALTER
          So have I!

                    NORA
          Hush!

                    CLEM
               (to the Prices)
          Why do you stay, then? Doesn't it
          frighten you?

                    EILEEN
          Oh yes, it's terrifying.

                    IRMA
          Yes, most exhilarating.

EXT. BEACH - SUNSET

Clem climbs down a narrow path from the top of the cliff
to a narrow strip of beach below. The WAVES CRASH against
the sheer cliff face nearby, but here the WATER simply
BUBBLES up over the sand and recedes just as quietly.

Clem watches the tide come in and go out for a long time.

                    CLEM
          What am I looking for, Monty?

INT. BERGMAN MANOR - KITCHEN - NIGHT

Dorothy scrubs dishes in the sink.

Clem startles her when he walks in from the dining hall.

                    CLEM
          Oh, excuse me. I just... I
          wondered if I might have a little
          late night snack.

Dorothy dries her hands.

                    DOROTHY
          Yes, sir. What can I get for you?

                    CLEM
          Milk and cookies?

                    DOROTHY
          How daring of you.

But she makes her way to the icebox and pulls out the
milk.

Clem helps himself to a seat as Dorothy sets a glass and
a plate of cookies in front of him. She pours the milk.

                    CLEM
          Thank you.

                    DOROTHY
          You don't mind if I continue my
          work?

She dives back into the dirty dishes.

                    CLEM
          Of course not. If you don't mind
          me sitting here while you do.

                    DOROTHY
          You're a guest. You may do
          whatever you please.

                    CLEM
          Whatever I please. There must be
          guests who take that invitation to
          heart.

                    DOROTHY
          I don't know what you mean, sir.

                    CLEM
          Don't you?

Dorothy stops what she's doing.

                    CLEM (CONT'D)
          No, I guess not. How long have you
          worked here, Dorothy?

                    DOROTHY
          As long as I can remember.

She turns from the dishes and faces Clem.

                    DOROTHY (CONT'D)
          I said they were rumors, but they
          weren't far wrong. Odin -- Mr.
          Bergman took me in as a child. I
          have no parents, no memories
          before Bergman Manor.

                    CLEM
          And what do you make of all the
          rumors about Bergman Manor being
          haunted?

Dorothy seems uncomfortable.

                    DOROTHY
          Depends on which rumors you've
          heard.

                    CLEM
          Noises in the night. Shadows
          lurking around every corner.

Dorothy doesn't answer, lost in some frightening thought.

                    CLEM (CONT'D)
          Dorothy?

                    DOROTHY
          It's an old house.

Clem opens his mouth to ask another question, but:

                    DOROTHY (CONT'D)
          Put the glass in the sink and the
          milk back in the icebox when
          you're done, if you don't mind?
          Goodnight, sir.

Dorothy leaves, the rest of the dirty dishes forgotten.

INT. BERGMAN MANOR - CLEM'S ROOM - NIGHT

Clem sits at the small desk in the corner of the room. He
puffs on a pipe as he writes notes.

A BONE-CRUNCHING THUD, THUD, THUD catches his ear. It
GROWS LOUDER.

Clem slowly crosses the room to the door. He puts his ear
to the door and listens.

The THUDDING GETS LOUDER and LOUDER. When it's almost
UNBEARABLY LOUD, it suddenly STOPS with a CRACK.

Clem jumps back. The only sound now is his own heavy
breathing. Until...

SOFT FOOTSTEPS make their way down the hallway. Clem
yanks open the door.

INT. BERGMAN MANOR - HALLWAY - SAME

Clem steps into the hallway.

A young woman dressed in a long, high-collared black dress sobs in front of a guest's door.

Clem can only see her in profile, but she looks familiar.

She turns to walk away, toward the end of the hallway.

Clem follows her.

CLEM

Excuse me, miss. Is everything all right?

She doesn't seem to hear him. Just continues walking.

Clem walks faster to catch up. He's almost caught up at the end of the hallway. He turns the corner.

The long stretch of hallway in front of him is empty. He looks all around him, but there's no sign of where she could have gone. He looks down at the floor.

WHAT HE SEES

A woman's footprints. In blood. They fade out of sight.

BACK TO SCENE

Clem does his best not to be scared out of his wits as he hurries back toward his room.

INT. BERGMAN MANOR - HALLWAY - EARLY MORNING

Clem comes out of his room, dressed for the day. The rest of the house is quiet.

EXT. BERGMAN MANOR - MOMENTS LATER

Although the sun is just beginning to rise, it looks like it's going to be a beautiful day.

Clem comes out the front door.

EXT. BERGMAN MANOR - GARDEN - MOMENTS LATER

Clem takes his time walking through the garden. He stops in front of a particular hedge of bushes. He takes out Monty's old photo from his pocket and compares. It's the same hedge.

He puts the photo away and continues. As he comes around the hedge of bushes, he finds the GROUNDS KEEPER raking the pathway.

                    GROUNDS KEEPER
          Good morning, sir. Anything I can
          do for you?

                    CLEM
          It is a lovely morning, isn't it?
          What are you doing?

                    GROUNDS KEEPER
          The rain makes these terrible ruts
          in the pathways. I gotta even 'em
          out before the master sees it.

                    CLEM
          Mr. Bergman?

                    GROUNDS KEEPER
          He's a particular one. Likes
          things neat and proper.

                    CLEM
          I see. I have to confess, I was a
          little nervous about coming here
          for my vacation.

                    GROUNDS KEEPER
          Why's that, sir?

                    CLEM
          Haven't there been two deaths here
          this summer? Seems like awful bad
          luck, but maybe that's just a lot
          of superstitious nonsense.

                    GROUNDS KEEPER
          Ain't good luck, that's for sure.

A WOMAN'S SCREAM comes from the house, interrupting the conversation before Clem can answer. Clem runs toward the house.

INT. BERGMAN MANOR - HALLWAY - MOMENTS LATER

As Clem tops the stairs, he sees most of the guests standing halfway in the hallway in their robes.

                    CLEM
          What's happened?

No one answers, but from a room at the end of the
hallway, he hears:

                    HORACE (O.S.)
          What have you done to my boy?!

                    DOROTHY (O.S.)
               (hysterical)
          It wasn't me!

Clem runs toward the commotion.

INT. BERGMAN MANOR - THOMAS'S ROOM - SAME

Clem rounds the corner just in time to see Horace
backhand Dorothy across the face. Odin grabs Horace by
the lapel and shoves him against the wall.

                    ODIN
          You keep your hands off her!

                    HORACE
          Let go of me!

They scuffle, and Clem rushes to separate them.

                    CLEM
          Calm down! Let go! Calm down!

Finally, he gets them apart.

Dorothy crouches against a wall, holding her face and
sobbing.

                    CLEM (CONT'D)
          Somebody tell me what the hell is
          going on here.

                    HORACE
          She killed my son!

Clem keeps a hand on Horace to hold him at bay and looks
around at the bed.

Sure enough, there's Thomas's cold, stiff body.

On the bedside table, a bottle of pills has tipped over
and spilled.

By now, the other guests have gathered around the door to
see what's going on.

                              EILEEN
                    Dr. Campbell!

She disappears.

                              IRMA
                    Poor Thomas!

Marie faints, and Arthur Tobin barely catches her before
she hits the floor.

                         DR. CAMPBELL (O.S.)
                    Excuse me, pardon me.

He shoves his way through the bodies crowding the doorway
and enters the room with his little black doctor's bag.
He goes to Thomas's body and begins his examination.

                              CLEM
                    Eileen, Irma. Please take Horace
                    and see that he gets a good,
                    strong cup of coffee.

The Price sisters hurry forward and reach for Horace, but
he shrugs them off.

                              HORACE
                    Like hell! That's my boy!

                              IRMA
                    Horace, please.

                              EILEEN
                    Please, Horace.

Horace points at Dorothy.

                              HORACE
                    I'm not leaving him here with her.

                              EILEEN
                    Of course not. She's leaving too.

                              IRMA
                    That's right. We're all leaving so
                    Dr. Campbell can do his work.

Horace is still reluctant, but the Price sisters get the
job done.

Clem helps Dorothy off the floor.

                              CLEM
                    Are you all right?

Dorothy's still crying, but she nods her head.

                    CLEM (CONT'D)
          Mr. Bergman.

Odin understands and leads Dorothy from the room.

Dr. Campbell picks up one of the pills and inspects it.

Clem turns his attention to the other patrons still
gathered at the door.

                    CLEM (CONT'D)
          Please, go back to your rooms. I
          think the good doctor will be able
          to work better without all of us
          here to disturb him.

They disperse. Clem shuts the door behind them and turns
back to Dr. Campbell.

                    DR. CAMPBELL
          You didn't have to send them away.
          Nothing I can do here. The boy's
          dead.
               (beat)
          They only think I'm hard of
          hearing.

Clem smiles.

                    CLEM
          I'll remember that. Do you know
          what killed him?

                    DR. CAMPBELL
          For certain, no. But by the looks
          of it, overdose.

                    CLEM
          Why would Horace accuse the girl?

                    DR. CAMPBELL
          Everyone pretended not to notice,
          but Thomas and Dorothy had a habit
          of... disappearing at the same
          time.

                    CLEM
          They were lovers?

                    DR. CAMPBELL
          I'm just a humble doctor. What do
          I know of such things?

INT. BERGMAN MANOR - KITCHEN - SAME

Dorothy sits with a cold cloth pressed to her cheek. Odin bends in front of her and gently moves the cloth away.

> ODIN
> Let's see it.

Odin touches the already bruising skin tenderly. Dorothy flinches.

> ODIN (CONT'D)
> That bastard.

> DOROTHY
> I don't care much for Mr. Cooper, but the poor man just lost his son. I'm sure he wasn't thinking clearly.

> ODIN
> That doesn't give him the right to beat innocent girls.

> DOROTHY
> Who says I'm innocent?

The comment bothers Odin.

> ODIN
> Anyway, you certainly didn't kill the boy.

> DOROTHY
> No, I didn't kill Thomas.

INT. BERGMAN MANOR - UPPER FLOOR - DAY

Someone watches through a window as Thomas's body is loaded into an ambulance. Horace climbs into a car behind the ambulance, and the caravan pulls away.

A black car remains in the drive. Two detectives converse with Odin next to it. After a moment, they all shake hands, and the detectives climb into the car and drive away.

Odin walks back into the house.

EXT. BERGMAN MANOR - CLIFF - SAME

A stone bench looks out over the steep cliff. Madame
Guillaume sits on the bench. Marie stands near the
cliff's edge, staring at the sea.

Clem approaches.

                    CLEM
          Good afternoon.

Madame Guillaume turns to look at him, but Marie ignores
him.

                    MADAME GUILLAUME
          Ah, good afternoon. Marie, don't
          be rude.

Marie finally turns and nods her greeting.

Clem takes a seat on the bench next to Madame.

                    CLEM
          You don't mind if I join you? It's
          such a beautiful view.

                    MADAME GUILLAUME
          Beautiful and terrifying. I don't
          know how she stands so close to
          the edge.

                    CLEM
          She is your daughter?

                    MADAME GUILLAUME
          You flatter beautifully. Marie is
          my granddaughter. You'll have to
          excuse her -- how do you say --
          melancholy. The death of that
          young man has upset her very much.
          I think we may cut our trip short
          if she does not recover.

                    CLEM
          Did she know Thomas well?

                    MADAME GUILLAUME
          Just well enough to want to know
          him better, I think.

Marie turns.

MARIE
You talk about me as if I'm not
even here.

MADAME GUILLAUME
Marie, you are being very rude.

CLEM
No, she's right. My apologies,
Marie. I was told you didn't speak
English, otherwise I would have
addressed you directly.

MARIE
The Price sisters told you that.

CLEM
Yes.

MARIE
It is because you are attractive,
and they want to keep you for
themselves. It's what they always
do.

CLEM
Always?

MADAME GUILLAUME
We have come here every summer
since Marie was eight years old.
The Prices also come every summer.

CLEM
Who else comes every summer?

MADAME GUILLAUME
The Tobins and the Campbells.

CLEM
The Campbells?

MADAME GUILLAUME
Ah, pardon. Dr. Campbell. He used
to come with his wife every
summer, but she died two, three
years ago. He still comes. I think
we are like his family now.

CLEM
Do you come for the thrill of
staying in a haunted mansion like
the Prices do?

                    MADAME GUILLAUME
          I'll admit, there is something
          strange about this place. But
          haunted? Children's stories,
          Monsieur Beauregard.

                    CLEM
          Is that what you think, Marie?

                    MARIE
          I don't believe in ghosts, if
          that's what you mean. But I do
          think there is something, or
          someone, else that haunts this
          place.

                    MADAME GUILLAUME
          Come now, Marie. Don't be
          childish.

                    MARIE
          It's not childish. You know,
          monsieur, Thomas is not the first
          man to die here.

                    CLEM
          Everyone knows that.

                    MARIE
          The man who died earlier this
          summer. He is supposed to have
          fallen off this cliff.

                    CLEM
          You think something else happened?

                    MADAME GUILLAUME
          This is nonsense. I saw his body
          on the rocks down there myself.

                    MARIE
          Yes, he fell. But I don't believe
          it was an accident like they say.

                    CLEM
          And the man who died earlier this
          week?

                    MARIE
          He drowned. Right down there.

She points to the beach below.

                    MARIE (CONT'D)
          He asked a lot of questions. Like
          you.

Clem smiles.

                    CLEM
          And Thomas?

                    MARIE
          Thomas did not want to kill
          himself.

                    CLEM
          How do you know?

Marie looks at her grandmother, wondering if she should
speak.

                    MARIE
          Thomas and I were planning to run
          away together.

Clem is genuinely surprised. But not as surprised as
Madame Guillaume.

                    MADAME GUILLAUME
          Marie!

                    MARIE
          I'm sorry, Grandmama. We had
          planned to leave last night. I was
          to meet him in the garage. We
          would take his father's car. When
          he didn't come, I waited. For
          hours I waited. Finally, when it
          was almost dawn, I thought he must
          have changed his mind or been
          detained by his father. It was
          only an hour later that the maid
          discovered his body.

Madame Guillaume fans herself, trying to recover from the
shock of her granddaughter's story.

                    CLEM
          Forgive me for asking, Marie, but
          did anyone else know of your plan?

                    MARIE
          The cook, Mrs. O'Toole. I believe
          she may have seen us together. And
          I believe she may have told the
          maid.

                         CLEM
          Why do you say that?

                         MARIE
          I'm no fool, Monsieur Beauregard.
          I saw the way the maid looked at
          Thomas. She was in love with him.

                         CLEM
          Dr. Campbell seemed to think
          Thomas was quite fond of her as
          well.

                         MARIE
          He flirted with her. Nothing more.

                         CLEM
          And that didn't bother you?

                         MARIE
          It diverted attention away from
          me. If Monsieur Cooper had known
          about Thomas and me, he would have
          tried to stop us.

                         CLEM

          Why?

                         MADAME GUILLAUME
          Thomas was engaged to another
          woman, Monsieur Beauregard. And I
          assure you, if I had known, I
          would have put a stop to the
          affair as well.

                         CLEM
          Thomas was a busy man.

INT. BERGMAN MANOR - THOMAS'S ROOM - LATER

Clem inspects the drawers, the bed, everything. He gets
on his hands and knees and looks under the bed. He sees
the crumpled up note. He only has it halfway open when...

Dorothy enters with her arms full of fresh linens.

                         DOROTHY
               Oh!

Clem turns at the sound of her voice. He hides the note
behind his back.

>   DOROTHY (CONT'D)
>   What are you doing in here? And
>   what do you have behind your back?

>   CLEM
>   Nothing. I was just... curious, I
>   suppose.

>   DOROTHY
>   Show it to me, or I'll call Mr.
>   Bergman and have him throw you out
>   for being a thief.

Clem holds up the crumpled paper.

>   CLEM
>   It's just a piece of paper I
>   dropped. See?

He nods at the linens.

>   CLEM (CONT'D)
>   Isn't it a little soon for that?

>   DOROTHY
>   The detectives said they had
>   gathered all the evidence they
>   could here.

>   CLEM
>   And what about you?

>   DOROTHY
>   What about me?

>   CLEM
>   It doesn't bother you to change
>   your lover's sheets the same day
>   you discovered his dead body?

His words hurt.

>   CLEM (CONT'D)
>   You were the one who discovered
>   him, weren't you?

>   DOROTHY
>   He wasn't my lover.

>   CLEM
>   No?

                    DOROTHY
          Thomas flirted with me. He may
          have even kissed me once or twice.
          But we never -- I never --

                    CLEM
          What were you doing in his room so
          early this morning?

                    DOROTHY
          Not what you're thinking. Thomas
          had a standing order for an early
          wake up call every morning. This
          morning, when he didn't respond, I
          grew worried.

Clem sees sincerity in her face. He believes her.

                    CLEM
          My apologies.

He motions for her to go about her business, and she
does. Clem is about to leave, but:

                    DOROTHY
          And yes. It does bother me.

Clem stops. He watches her work for a moment.

                    CLEM
          You must have known the other men
          who died here too.

                    DOROTHY
          The other men?

                    CLEM
          Five in the last five years? Six,
          counting Thomas. Three just this
          summer.

                    DOROTHY
          Sure I did. As well as I know any
          guest, I suppose.

                    CLEM
          As well as you knew Thomas?

                    DOROTHY
          What are you implying, Mr.
          Beauregard?

                              CLEM
                    Nothing. Forgive me. I didn't mean
                    to pry.

Clem leaves Dorothy to her work.

INT. BERGMAN MANOR - CLEM'S ROOM - NIGHT

Clem puffs on his pipe and takes the note from Thomas's
room from his pocket. He reads the words:

"STAY AWAY FROM HER"

He hears SOFT FOOTSTEPS in the hallway again.

INT. BERGMAN MANOR - CLEM'S ROOM/HALLWAY - NIGHT

Clem opens the door. There's no one there. A SCRAPING
sound comes from below. Clem follows the sound, down the
hallway toward the stairs.

INT. BERGMAN MANOR - LIBRARY - MOMENTS LATER

The SCRAPING comes to a sudden STOP when Clem flips the
library light on. Clem stares in amazement.

WHAT HE SEES

The portrait of the woman is all askew, ripped to shreds.

CLEM

Looks around to see if anyone else might have heard. No
one else stirs.

He goes to the portrait and lifts a shred to complete the
woman's lovely face. Suddenly it clicks...

MEMORY FLASH

The woman sobbing in the hallway.

                                        END FLASHBACK.

Clem, horrified, trips over himself as he backs away from
the portrait. He shakes all over.

EXT. BERGMAN MANOR - LAWN - DAY

The Tobin boys kick a ball around while their parents enjoy coffee and sandwiches in the gazebo with the Price sisters.

INT. BERGMAN MANOR - LIBRARY - SAME

Dr. Campbell reads a book near the window.

EXT. BERGMAN MANOR - GARDEN - SAME

Madame Guillaume walks through the garden chattering away at Odin, who listens patiently. Marie follows more slowly, looking terribly sad.

EXT. BEACH - SAME

Samuel and Lillian walk arm-in-arm, lovey-dovey as ever.

INT. BERGMAN MANOR - CLEM'S ROOM - SAME

Dorothy finishes making the bed. She sweeps pipe ash and spilled tobacco from the desk. Something catches her eye.

She moves aside the tobacco pouch and the ashtray. Underneath is Clem's notebook, with newspaper articles and the old photograph stuck in between pages.

Looking around to make sure hers are the only prying eyes, Dorothy opens to the first page.

INT. BERGMAN MANOR - KITCHEN - SAME

Clem pokes his head in from the dining hall. Mrs. O'Toole is hard at work.

                    CLEM
          I beg your pardon. May I bother
          you for a bicarbonate of soda?

                    MRS. O'TOOLE
          Of course.

Clem comes in, and Mrs. O'Toole fills a glass with water and stirs in bicarbonate of soda. The stuff fizzes. She hands it to Clem.

>   MRS. O'TOOLE (CONT'D)
>   You must be him.

Clem gulps down the liquid.

>   CLEM
>   Who's that?

>   MRS. O'TOOLE
>   The nosy one with nice hair.

Clem raises his eyebrows.

>   MRS. O'TOOLE (CONT'D)
>   Don't act so surprised. Servants
>   talk too, you know.

Clem smiles.

>   CLEM
>   You can tell her I think she has
>   nice hair too.

Now it's Mrs. O'Toole's turn to raise her eyebrows.

>   CLEM (CONT'D)
>   Was Mr. Bergman very upset about
>   the portrait in the library?

>   MRS. O'TOOLE
>   Whatever do you mean?

>   CLEM
>   The portrait in the library. It
>   was destroyed last night.

>   MRS. O'TOOLE
>   Destroyed!

Mrs. O'Toole rushes from the kitchen. Clem follows her.

INT. BERGMAN MANOR - LIBRARY - SAME

Mrs. O'Toole and Clem burst in, disturbing Dr. Campbell's
reading.

>   DR. CAMPBELL
>   What's this?

Clem can't believe it: the portrait is in perfect
condition. He goes to touch it, run his fingers over it.
Not a scratch.

                         CLEM
          But last night...

                         MRS. O'TOOLE
          Daft, you are.

INT. BERGMAN MANOR - FOYER - MOMENTS LATER

Clem walks through the foyer, bewildered by what he's
just seen.

Dorothy, just reaching the bottom of the stairs, catches
him by the arm and stops him.

                         DOROTHY
          We need to talk.

                         CLEM
          Okay.

                         DOROTHY
          Not here.

Dorothy grabs Clem by the hand and leads him upstairs.

INT. BERGMAN MANOR - HALLWAY - MOMENTS LATER

Dorothy leads Clem through the hallway to his own door.

                         CLEM
          But this is my room.

Dorothy doesn't respond, just opens the door and leads
him inside.

INT. BERGMAN MANOR - CLEM'S ROOM - SAME

Dorothy goes directly to the small desk and picks up
Clem's notebook.

                         DOROTHY
          What is this?

                         CLEM
          My private journal. But I'm
          guessing that didn't stop you from
          looking inside.

                         DOROTHY
          There's a list of all the guests
          and notes about all of them.
                         (MORE)

                              DOROTHY (CONT'D)
                    And about me and Odin. And
                    articles about Bergman Manor. Why?

          Clem rips the notebook out of her hand.

                              CLEM
                    That's the luxury of a private
                    journal. You can write about
                    whatever interests you. The people
                    here interest me.

                              DOROTHY
                    And Thomas's death. And the deaths
                    of the other men. You seem very
                    interested in those as well. Are
                    you a journalist? A detective? Who
                    do you work for?

                              CLEM
                    No one.

                              DOROTHY
                    Shall we see if Mr. Bergman
                    believes you?

          She starts toward the door. Clem stops her.

                              CLEM
                    My uncle was J. Alan Montgomery,
                    the man who died here earlier this
                    week. I came here to find out what
                    happened to him.

                              DOROTHY
                    Didn't the police tell you what
                    happened?

                              CLEM
                    Yes, but... I'm not convinced it
                    was an accident or suicide or
                    whatever they think. And I'm not
                    convinced about Thomas either. Or
                    the other men.

          Dorothy is silent, trying to decide whether to trust him.
          Clem flips to the very back of his notebook and pulls out
          Thomas's crumpled note.

                              CLEM (CONT'D)
                    Did you see this when you went
                    snooping through my things?

          He hands it to her, and she reads it.

                    DOROTHY
          What is this?

                    CLEM
          I found it in Thomas's room.

Dorothy covers her mouth and tears up.

                    DOROTHY
          Oh no.

                    CLEM
          What?

                    DOROTHY
          It's my fault. All of them are.

                    CLEM
          What do you mean?

                    DOROTHY
          This note. It's about me.

                    CLEM
          How do you know? Thomas was
          carrying on with Marie too. Maybe
          that note is about her.

                    DOROTHY
          He was what?

                    CLEM
          You didn't know?

                    DOROTHY
          I should've known. That sheik.
          Still... I'm sure the note is
          about me.

                    CLEM
          Why?

                    DOROTHY
          Because it happens every time. All
          the others... the ones who died.
          They were all stuck on me. Only,
          not your uncle. I never even spoke
          to him.

Clem is thoughtful for a moment.

                    CLEM
          I've been trying to figure out
          what he had in common with the
          rest of them, but maybe that's the
          wrong question. Maybe he figured
          out who the murderer is, and
          that's why he died.

                    DOROTHY
          Murder. Golly. I guess I've always
          suspected it, but I've never said
          it out loud.

                    CLEM
          You must have an idea who's behind
          all this. Who has an interest in
          keeping men away from you.

Dorothy doesn't answer for a long time.

                    DOROTHY
          There's something else you should
          know.

Clem waits.

                    DOROTHY (CONT'D)
          Every time someone dies, I hear
          something.

                    CLEM
          What do you hear?

                    DOROTHY
          I don't know, it's like a
          pounding, or a thudding. It's hard
          to explain.

Clem's eyes go wide.

                    CLEM
          You heard it the night Thomas
          died?

Dorothy nods.

                    CLEM (CONT'D)
          I heard it too. I went to look...
          the woman. Who's the woman in the
          portrait in the library?

Dorothy is confused by the quick change of subject.

                    DOROTHY
          Agnes. Agnes Bergman. Odin's
          sister. She died --

                    CLEM
          Twenty years ago. Committed
          suicide. Supposedly.

Dorothy nods again. They're both quiet for a moment.

                    DOROTHY
               (whispers)
          Do you think it's her?

INT. BERGMAN MANOR - HALLWAY - MOMENTS LATER

Odin, Dr. Campbell, and the Guillaumes are just mounting
the stairs when Clem's door opens, and Clem and Dorothy
both emerge. Spotting the group, Dorothy puts her head
down and hurries toward the opposite end of the hall, but
Clem walks toward the stairs.

He looks embarrassed when he sees Odin and the guests.
Odin looks at him darkly.

                    CLEM
          Hiya.

                    DR. CAMPBELL
          Mr. Beauregard.

Clem heads down the stairs.

INT. BERGMAN MANOR - SERVANTS' QUARTERS - MOMENTS LATER

Dorothy comes out of her room and almost runs into Odin,
who's waiting for her. It startles her.

                    ODIN
          Moving on already?

                    DOROTHY
          I don't know what you mean.

                    ODIN
          Don't you? You represent this
          establishment, Dorothy. When you
          make a fool of yourself, you make
          a fool of me.

                         DOROTHY
               Then you have nothing to worry
               about.

Odin grabs her arm and squeezes. It clearly hurts, but it
only makes her more defiant.

                         ODIN
               Don't pretend with me. What were
               you doing in his room?

Dorothy smiles through the pain.

                         DOROTHY
               What a good servant is supposed to
               do. Keeping the customers happy.

She tears free of his grip and walks away.

INT. BERGMAN MANOR - CLEM'S ROOM - NIGHT

Clem reads the account of Agnes's death in the newspaper
clipping.

Words come IN and OUT of FOCUS: "jumped off the cliff",
"left a suicide note for her brother", "was still in
mourning for her late father, Franz Bergman".

Clem compares the date on the article to Monty's old
photograph.

                         CLEM
               The same summer, maybe. Did you
               see something that summer, Monty?
               Is that why you came back here?

Suddenly, the BONE-CRUNCHING THUD, THUD, THUD begins. It
makes Clem jump.

INT. BERGMAN MANOR - HALLWAY - NIGHT

It's very dark until a sliver of light from Clem's room
cuts across the hallway.

The THUD, THUD, THUD BEATS steadily.

Clem steps into the hallway and shuts his door silently
behind him. He follows the sound.

MYSTERY POV

Follows Clem's movements from around a corner. There's NO THUDDING from this POV.

INT. BERGMAN MANOR - SERVANTS' QUARTERS - NIGHT

Clem reaches the servants' quarters. The THUDDING is LOUDER here, but he still can't find the source.

A door opens next to Clem, startling him. It's Dorothy in her nightgown and robe. She hears it too.

                    DOROTHY
          You shouldn't --

Clem puts a finger to his lips, hushing her.

A shadow passes at the end of the hallway, scaring them both.

                    DOROTHY (CONT'D)
               (whispers)
          You saw that, right?

Clem walks toward the end of the hallway.

                    DOROTHY (CONT'D)
          Clem, wait! Don't go after it!

But he's determined. Dorothy tiptoes after him.

INT. BERGMAN MANOR - UPPER FLOOR - NIGHT

Clem and Dorothy reach the upper floor. The THUDDING SUDDENLY STOPS.

                    CLEM
          Where's the light?

                    DOROTHY
          There's no electricity in this
          room. Only gaslights.

Clem takes a match from his pocket and strikes it. He finds a wall-mounted gaslight nearby. He lights it and turns it as high as it will go.

They stand in a room cluttered with dusty, cobwebbed furniture and boxes.

                              DOROTHY (CONT'D)
          Look.

Dorothy points.

In the middle of the floor a puddle of water blossoms
from nowhere, and in the middle of the puddle, something
gold and shiny.

Clem picks it up and inspects it: it's a cuff link with
the letter "B" on it.

                              CLEM
          Bergman.

Dorothy and Clem exchange looks.

INT. BERGMAN MANOR - SERVANTS' QUARTERS - NIGHT

Clem escorts Dorothy to her room. She turns at her door.

                              DOROTHY
                    (whispers)
          Clem...

Clem looks at her and smiles.

                              CLEM
          I like it when you call me by my
          first name.

                              DOROTHY
          Mr. Beauregard. I want you to
          leave Bergman Manor.

                              CLEM
          Excuse me?

                              DOROTHY
          You're not safe here.

Clem smiles again.

                              CLEM
          Because of you?

                              DOROTHY
          I'm serious.

                              CLEM
          So am I.

He leans over and kisses her. She doesn't resist, but she doesn't respond either.

                    CLEM (CONT'D)
          Goodnight, Dorothy.

He leaves, and she shuts her door with a worried expression on her face.

INT. BERGMAN MANOR - CLEM'S ROOM - MOMENTS LATER

Clem comes in and flips on the light. His breath catches.

There on his pillow is a note, just like Thomas's:

"STAY AWAY FROM HER"

INT. BERGMAN MANOR - FOYER - MORNING

Clem comes down the stairs and heads for the dining hall. Before he can get there, Odin calls from the library.

                    ODIN
          Mr. Beauregard. Good morning.

                    CLEM
          Good morning.

                    ODIN
          I'm having my breakfast in the
          library this morning. Will you
          join me?

                    CLEM
          It would be a pleasure.

INT. BERGMAN MANOR - LIBRARY - LATER

Odin and Clem sit at a small table near the window. Dorothy sets breakfast in front of them.

Clem glances at her, but she avoids his gaze.

                    CLEM
          Thank you.

Dorothy bows and leaves without making eye contact.

Clem sips at his coffee and forks food into his mouth. Odin stares at him and doesn't touch his own food.

                    ODIN
          I've been meaning to thank you for
          your help with the incident
          earlier this week.

Clem looks up from his meal.

                    ODIN (CONT'D)
          I'm not sure what Horace might
          have done if you hadn't come in
          when you did.

                    CLEM
          Or what you might have done.

Odin smiles. But it's creepy.

                    ODIN
          Most of my patrons are what you
          might call regulars. They spend
          every summer here. The Selmers
          have been here several weeks now.
          I wouldn't be a bit surprised if
          they come back next summer and
          every summer after that.

                    CLEM
          Speaks well of a business that has
          such loyal customers.

                    ODIN
          Yes. But I'm afraid we've made a
          rather poor first impression on
          you.

                    CLEM
          I have no complaints.

                    ODIN
          Plenty of questions though, it
          would seem.

Clem freezes.

                    ODIN (CONT'D)
          Is that what kept you and Dorothy
          occupied so long in your room
          yesterday? Maybe you were asking
          her about the ghost of Bergman
          Manor?

                    CLEM
          I don't believe in ghost stories,
          Mr. Bergman.

Odin smiles again, and Clem is unsettled by it.

Suddenly, Irma appears in the doorway.

                    IRMA
          Eileen! Eileen, I've found him!
          Odin's been monopolizing him.

Eileen appears behind Irma, and they both come bouncing
over.

                    EILEEN
          Clem Beauregard, you promised to
          make things more interesting
          around here, but we've hardly seen
          you.

Clem stands.

                    CLEM
          Shame on me. Ladies, today, I am
          all yours.

The Prices squeal with delight.

                    CLEM (CONT'D)
          You'll excuse me, Mr. Bergman.

Odin nods.

Clem lets Eileen and Irma lead him out of the room.

                    IRMA
          Do you know anything about
          sailing?

                    CLEM
          I used to go sailing with my uncle
          as a boy.

                    EILEEN
          Perfect!

EXT. SAILBOAT - DAY

Clem pulls in the sail and heaves the anchor.

Eileen pours champagne into three glasses.

The boat bobs on the edge of the small cove overlooked by
the sheer cliff on which Bergman Manor sits.

Eileen passes out the champagne as Clem takes a seat between the sisters.

                    EILEEN
          Real French champagne. I found it
          in Madame Guillaume's room.

                    IRMA
          Isn't this just the most lovely
          spot? Eileen and I bring all our
          victims here, you know.

                    CLEM
          I don't doubt it.

                    EILEEN
          Ugh, I'm so glad to be rid of
          those awful Tobins.

                    IRMA
          Oh yes, what a drag. If you ask
          me, people should never have
          children. They become so boring
          once they have the responsibility
          of taking care of those little
          monsters.

                    CLEM
          The human race wouldn't last very
          long if everyone thought that way.

                    EILEEN
          Oh, but it would be so much more
          fun while it lasted.

Irma and Eileen clink their glasses and drink on it.

                    CLEM
          Anyway, I thought you got on with
          the Tobins quite well.

                    EILEEN
          Well, the parents are all right, I
          suppose.

                    IRMA
          Especially when the options are so
          limited. Since poor Thomas died
          and Horace left, you and the
          Tobins are the only real people
          left.

                    CLEM
          What about the Selmers?

                    IRMA
          They haven't spoken a word to
          anyone since they arrived. I don't
          think they've even noticed there
          are other people here.

                    CLEM
          And Mr. Bergman? You must like him
          well enough to come back every
          summer.

                    IRMA
          Odin? Ha!

Clem doesn't get it.

                    EILEEN
          Odin is hardly what one would call
          entertaining company. He's a
          competent proprietor, I grant you.
          But socially speaking, he's a
          terrible bore.

Clem drains his champagne and stands.

                    CLEM
          Well, I promised you excitement.
          Shall we swim?

He strips down to his bathing suit and jumps into the
water.

Irma and Eileen do the same.

INT. BERGMAN MANOR - HALLWAY - SAME

Dorothy looks around and knocks softly on Clem's door. No
answer. She tries the handle and pushes the door open
just enough to peek inside.

INT. BERGMAN MANOR - CLEM'S ROOM - SAME

It's empty, of course. Dorothy shuts the door quietly.

INT. BERGMAN MANOR - KITCHEN - MOMENTS LATER

Dorothy enters just as Mrs. O'Toole sets the last plate
of food on the serving tray.

                    DOROTHY
          You can take three of those away.

                    MRS. O'TOOLE
          Ah? Who's missing lunch today?

Mrs. O'Toole removes three of the plates from the tray.

                    DOROTHY
          The Price sisters and Cle-- Mr.
          Beauregard.

Dorothy lifts the serving tray and takes it away.

Mrs. O'Toole watches after her and shakes her head.

EXT. WATER - SAME

Clem and the Prices splash in the water and take turns
dunking each other. The Prices team up on Clem and push
his head under, but something under the water happens,
and they squeal and let him up.

Clem eyes a group of giant rocks that jut out of the
water at the base of the cliff.

                    CLEM
          Race to the rocks?

                    IRMA
          Heavens, no!

                    CLEM
          I'll give you a twenty yard
          handicap. And swim with my hands
          behind my back, only kicking my
          feet.

                    EILEEN
          It isn't that, Clem. We don't dare
          go near those rocks.

                    IRMA
          It gives me the willies just
          thinking about it.

                    CLEM
          Why? What's wrong?

                    EILEEN
          They say that's where Odin's
          sister died.

                    IRMA
          And don't forget that poor young
          man at the beginning of the
          summer.

                    EILEEN
          Oh, yes, that was just awful. What
          if there are still... you know...
          parts?

                    CLEM
          Oh, come now. You aren't really
          afraid of the rocks?

                    IRMA
          Don't you know, Clem? Odin's
          sister is the one who haunts the
          house. No, I don't dare go near
          the spot where she died.

All the childish joy of the afternoon dissipates. Clem
looks again at the rocks as he considers Irma and
Eileen's story.

Clem visibly shivers. But he's gotta know more.

He swims toward the rock.

                    EILEEN
          Clem, don't!

                    IRMA
          Clem, come back! Clem!

Their voices fade as he swims away from them.

EXT. ROCKS - SAME

Clem heaves himself up onto the jagged rocks and looks
around. Water flows in between the rocks, rising and
receding with each wave. He looks back at Irma and Eileen
in the distance and waves to let them know he's all
right.

He picks his way over rocks, being careful not to slip on
the wet surface. He catches sight of something a few
rocks away, and makes his way over.

What he finds is a shred of black fabric. He yanks it
free.

MEMORY FLASH

The woman sobbing in the hallway. The hem of her long,
black dress is torn and ragged.

END FLASHBACK.

Clem shivers again. He looks around, and deep in a
crevice, something gold and shiny gleams in the sunlight.

Clem reaches down to grab it, but the crevice is too deep
and narrow for his hand. His fingers just brush it.

A wave comes in, causing water to pool around him. The
rising water lifts the shiny object just enough.

Clem barely holds onto it between two fingertips and
wiggles to get it out from between the rocks. Finally, he
has it free.

It's a cuff link. It matches the one from the upper room.
The "B" on it is more faded, but still legible.

EXT. BERGMAN MANOR - GARDEN - LATE AFTERNOON

Clem's hair is still wet from his swim, but he's dressed.
He's about to turn toward the front door when he hears
angry voices on the other side of the hedge. He stops and
listens.

                    DOROTHY (O.S.)
          Just because you pay me doesn't
          mean you own me, Odin. You can't
          tell me who to --

                    ODIN (O.S.)
          Yes I can. And I will. You'll stay
          away from him or --

                    DOROTHY (O.S.)
          Or what?

                    ODIN (O.S.)
          You think I won't fire you,
          Dorothy. You think you're above
          the rules just because I took you
          in when your whore mother left you
          with nothing.

Silence.

                         ODIN (O.S.) (CONT'D)
                    Don't take my generosity for
                    granted. I owe you nothing.

Clem waits to hear ODIN'S FOOTSTEPS FADE before coming
around the hedge.

He finds Dorothy sitting on a bench with her face in her
hands. Clem sits next to Dorothy.

                         DOROTHY
                    I don't want your apology.

                         CLEM
                    Good. I wasn't going to offer one.

Dorothy looks up. She was clearly expecting Odin.

                         DOROTHY
                    I'm sorry. Odin -- Mr. Bergman and
                    I were just --

                         CLEM
                    I know. I heard... enough.

Dorothy looks embarrassed.

Clem pulls a flower from the bush behind them and hands
it to Dorothy.

                         CLEM (CONT'D)
                    Was he talking about me?

                         DOROTHY
                    What does it matter. He's right.
                    He doesn't owe me anything. And I
                    owe him so much.

Clem pulls the cuff link from his vest pocket and shows
it to Dorothy.

                         CLEM
                    I found it on the rocks below.

                         DOROTHY
                    It matches the one we found
                    upstairs.

                         CLEM
                    Yup.

                         DOROTHY
                    What do you think it means?

                         CLEM
              Have you ever seen Odin wear cuff
              links like this?

                         DOROTHY
              Odin?

Clem pulls out the note he found in his bedroom.

                         CLEM
              This was on my pillow when I got
              back to my room last night.

Dorothy looks at Clem apologetically.

                         CLEM (CONT'D)
              And when Odin called me into the
              library this morning, he wanted to
              know what you were doing in my
              room yesterday.

                         DOROTHY
              It's not him, Clem. It's not.

                         CLEM
              Don't let your gratitude or
              loyalty or whatever this is...
              don't let it blind you.

                         DOROTHY
              Odin warned me to stay away from
              you because he's worried about the
              Manor's reputation. You heard him.
              He'd sooner fire me than get rid
              of a paying customer. Anyway, I
              don't understand what the cuff
              links have to do with any of it.

                         CLEM
              They're evidence.

                         DOROTHY
              Of what? We found one in a puddle
              upstairs, and you found its mate
              on the rocks down there. What is
              that evidence of? That someone --
              maybe Odin, maybe someone else --
              lost their cuff links. That's all
              you can possibly know from those.

Clem deflates, knowing she's right.

                    CLEM
          My uncle was right, you know. I
          don't have what it takes to be a
          private investigator.

Dorothy looks up at him, waits for him to continue.

                    CLEM (CONT'D)
          The cuff links, the photograph,
          the threatening notes... I have
          all these pieces, but no idea how
          any of them fit together. They
          make no sense. The portrait and
          the sound and --

                    DOROTHY
          Clem. We both heard the sound last
          night.

                    CLEM
          Yeah?

                    DOROTHY
          But no one died.

Clem thinks a moment, and then with chilling certainty:

                    CLEM
          Maybe someone was supposed to.

HIGH ABOVE

From a window on the upper floor, the curtains drop back
into place. Someone's been watching.

DOWN BELOW

A CLAP OF THUNDER and a couple of drops of rain force an
end to their conversation. They hurry together toward the
front door, Clem doing his best to shelter both of them
with his jacket as a few drops turns quickly into a
downpour.

INT. BERGMAN MANOR - FOYER - SAME

Just inside, Clem and Dorothy shake the water from their
clothes and hair.

Their eyes meet. It's electric. Clem moves toward
Dorothy, but she steps away.

                    DOROTHY
          Please leave me alone, Clem.
          Please.

She hurries off.

INT. BERGMAN MANOR - LIBRARY - EVENING

Rain pours down the windowpanes.

Dr. Campbell plays cards with the Guillaumes.

Eileen and Irma play a raucous game of charades with the
Tobins and the Selmers.

INT. BERGMAN MANOR - FOYER - SAME

Clem comes down the stairs silently, peeking inside the
library to make sure no one is missing him. He heads
toward a hallway that leads behind the stairs.

INT. BERGMAN MANOR - ODIN'S OFFICE - SAME

Clem pokes his head inside the cozy, cramped office. He
enters and casts one last glance outside before silently
shutting the door.

He starts with the desk. He looks through the papers on
top, and finding nothing interesting there, he sits and
opens drawers.

Across from him, a small, leather-bound book falls from a
shelf.

He looks up.

Clem rounds the desk and picks up the book. He opens to
the first page. The words are handwritten.

"The private journal of Franz Bergman May 1901 - October
1902"

Clem flips through the pages and stops on a random one:

"July 18, 1901

The day has finally arrived. Odin is leaving for Oxford.
All the guests will help us to see him off. I believe
dear Benjamin has even bought him a going away present. I
am so proud of Odin, as his mother would be if she could
see him today.

And yet, I know how much we shall miss him. Agnes loves him so. I only hope that helping me run the manor will divert her from her loneliness."

Clem snaps the book shut and stares at the spot on the shelf from which it fell. There's a whole collection of leather-bound books just like it.

VOICES outside the door, but still down the hall, tell Clem he needs to leave. He shoves the book back on the shelf and opens the door a crack.

INT. BERGMAN MANOR - LOWER HALLWAY - SAME

Odin has his back to the door, talking to Dorothy. Dorothy sees Clem's face.

                    ODIN
          Get it done. I don't care if you
          have to stay up all night.

He turns, but Dorothy catches his arm.

                    DOROTHY
     Wait.

                    ODIN
     What?

Clem squeezes out through the door and shuts it silently.

                    DOROTHY
          Um. I wanted to say... I'm sorry.

                    ODIN
     About what?

                    DOROTHY
          You know. About... Mr. Beauregard.

Clem tiptoes nearer to them, coming just behind Odin. He jerks his head toward the office, and Dorothy begins to walk that direction, keeping Odin's attention away. Clem stays behind Odin's back as he turns.

                    DOROTHY (CONT'D)
          You were right, and I'm sorry.

                    ODIN
     That's new.

Clem makes it free and clear as Odin follows Dorothy toward the office.

INT. BERGMAN MANOR - LIBRARY - SAME

Clem walks in just in time. Eileen drops the needle on
the phonograph and joins Irma dancing. Seeing Clem:

                    EILEEN
          Clem, dear, don't be such a bore.
          Come dance with us.

Clem smiles, takes Eileen in his arms, and dances with
her.

Irma dances alone as Arthur convinces Nora to join the
fun, and Samuel and Lillian give in too.

The song ends. As the next one begins, Clem releases
Eileen and approaches the card players. He offers a hand
to Marie.

                    CLEM
          May I?

She reluctantly accepts, and they dance.

Irma grabs Dr. Campbell. Eileen pulls a protesting Madame
Guillaume out of her seat, and the whole company dances.

Nora sits, having had enough, leaving Arthur without a
partner.

Clem takes a turn with Marie and notices Dorothy standing
in the doorway watching. He grabs the now-free Arthur and
hands Marie off. He makes his way over to Dorothy.

                    CLEM (CONT'D)
          Care to dance?

                    DOROTHY
          I hardly think it proper for the
          maid to dance with a guest.

                    CLEM
          Your job is to make my stay as
          pleasant and comfortable as
          possible, isn't it?

His smile is contagious, and she allows him to take her
into his arms and dance.

The other guests stare and murmur, but Clem and Dorothy
ignore them.

                         CLEM (CONT'D)
                    (whispers)
               Thank you for saving my skin out
               there.

Neither of them see Odin enter.

                         CLEM (CONT'D)
               I wanted to tell you that I found
               something --

                         ODIN
               Dorothy.

Dorothy pulls away from Clem immediately.

                         ODIN (CONT'D)
               Have you cleaned the windows in
               the garage yet?

                         DOROTHY
               It's after dark. And it's raining.

                         ODIN
               The rain won't stop you from
               cleaning them on the inside.

                         CLEM
               Mr. Bergman, surely the windows
               can wait. Would it hurt to let
               Dorothy enjoy herself?

                         ODIN
               She's a maid, Mr. Beauregard.

Dorothy glares at him, but she bites her tongue.

Odin takes a step closer and says in a low voice that
only she and Clem can hear:

                         ODIN (CONT'D)
               Don't make me ask again.

Dorothy leaves, humiliated.

INT. GARAGE - LATER

Dorothy scrubs a window pane on one of the garage doors.
She hears a CLATTERING from somewhere. She looks all
around her.

                         DOROTHY
               Hello? Is someone there?

No answer.

She throws her wet cloth into a bucket at her feet and uses a dry one draped over her shoulder to wipe the pane she's just cleaned.

The side door opens.

                    DOROTHY (CONT'D)
          Who's there?

Clem appears around the front of a car.

                    CLEM
          It's me.

Dorothy continues scrubbing.

                    DOROTHY
          You shouldn't be here.

                    CLEM
          I'm sorry about what happened in
          there.

                    DOROTHY
          You're tempting fate. Following me
          around, giving me flowers, dancing
          with me. But maybe that's what you
          mean to do.

                    CLEM
          What I mean to do?

Dorothy doesn't elaborate.

                    CLEM (CONT'D)
          I came out here to tell you what I
          found in Odin's office.

Dorothy stops scrubbing, but she doesn't look at Clem.

                    DOROTHY
          Are you using me, Clem? To solve
          your little mystery?

                    CLEM
          What?

                    DOROTHY
          You think it's Odin. And you think
          if you pretend to be stuck on me,
          you'll catch him out.

                         CLEM
          If you think I'm pretending,
          Dorothy, you've either
          overestimated my cleverness and
          cruelty or underestimated my
          feelings for you and my highly
          developed sense of self-
          preservation.

Dorothy moves onto the next window pane without
responding. Clem studies her. He grabs the dry cloth
draped over her shoulder and wipes down the window she's
just finished.

                         CLEM (CONT'D)
          Remember how I said before that I
          couldn't make all the pieces fit?
          What if Agnes's death is the key?
          Maybe Agnes didn't kill herself at
          all. Maybe she was murdered too.
          And if we can figure out what
          happened to her...

He has trouble spitting it out. Finally, Dorothy turns to
face him.

                         CLEM (CONT'D)
          I know it sounds wacky. But I
          can't shake the feeling that her
          death holds the answer.

                         DOROTHY
          What did you find?

                         CLEM
          Franz Bergman's journals. Odin's
          father. Agnes's father.

                         DOROTHY
          Franz died before Agnes did.

She goes back to scrubbing.

                         CLEM
          The answer is there. I know it is.

They continue in silence, Dorothy washing the windows,
and Clem drying them.

EXT. GARAGE - LATER

The rain continues to pour.

Clem comes out the side door. Something above him SCRAPES over the side of the roof.

He turns at the sound, just in time to see a roof tile hurtling down at him. He covers his head, and the TILE CRASHES on top of him.

He collapses.

Dorothy opens the door and sees him lying motionless at her feet.

> DOROTHY
> Clem!

INT. BERGMAN MANOR - CLEM'S ROOM - NIGHT

Clem's eyes flutter open. His hand goes to his head, which is wrapped with a bandage, and he winces.

> DR. CAMPBELL
> Pretty bad blow you took there,
> son. Had to give you a few
> stitches.

Dr. Campbell sits in a chair by Clem's bed. He holds up a finger.

> DR. CAMPBELL (CONT'D)
> Follow my finger.

He moves it back and forth, up and down. Clem's eyes follow without a problem.

> DR. CAMPBELL (CONT'D)
> How many fingers am I holding up?

He goes through a number of combinations.

> CLEM
> Two. Four. One.

> DR. CAMPBELL
> Good. You'll survive.

Dr. Campbell looks up.

> DR. CAMPBELL (CONT'D)
> See? Nothing to worry about.

Clem turns to see Dorothy standing in front of his desk, arms crossed, a worried expression on her face. Clem struggles to sit up.

Dr. Campbell stands.

                    DR. CAMPBELL (CONT'D)
          Don't keep him up too long. He
          needs rest.

He leaves, and Dorothy takes his place in the chair.

                    CLEM
          What time is it?

                    DOROTHY
          It's late. Everyone else went to
          bed more than an hour ago.

                    CLEM
          And you got stuck with nurse duty.

                    DOROTHY
          I didn't think you'd want anyone,
          even Dr. Campbell, to see all your
          notes and newspaper clippings.

She nods toward the desk.

                    DOROTHY (CONT'D)
          I managed to shove it all in a
          drawer during the commotion when
          Arthur and Dr. Campbell brought
          you in.

Clem smiles.

                    CLEM
          Thank you.

He scratches his head, displacing his bandage.

                    DOROTHY
          Be careful.

She leans over to adjust his bandage.

                    CLEM
          Ow!

He pulls her hands down, and his quick motion brings
their faces close together.

                    DOROTHY
          I'm sorry.

He doesn't let go. She doesn't move.

                    DOROTHY (CONT'D)
          Please let go of me. I'll be more
          gentle, I promise.

Clem complies, and Dorothy adjusts his bandage with care.

                    DOROTHY (CONT'D)
          I'm staying here tonight.

                    CLEM
          Are you making a pass at me, Miss
          Francis?

                    DOROTHY
          You're not safe.

Clem takes Dorothy's hand and rubs his thumb across her
fingers.

                    CLEM
          A week ago, I probably would have
          said yes. Especially if you were
          making a pass at me. But...

He brings her hand to his lips and kisses it.

                    CLEM (CONT'D)
          I won't risk your reputation for
          my safety. I do thank you kindly
          for the offer.

                    DOROTHY
          Clem, it's not a joke.

                    CLEM
          I know it's not. That tile was
          pushed. But somehow I think -- if
          falling for you is the reason I'm
          in danger -- I don't think your
          being in my room all night will
          help my cause.

Dorothy looks away, embarrassed.

                    CLEM (CONT'D)
          There is something you can do for
          me, though.

INT. BERGMAN MANOR - ODIN'S OFFICE - MOMENTS LATER

Dorothy uses an oil lamp to light her way. She searches
the shelves until she finds the collection of Franz
Bergman's journals. She grabs the last two on the shelf.

Suddenly, the DOOR SLAMS SHUT.

Dorothy runs to the door and yanks at the handle, but she's locked inside.

The BONE-CRUNCHING THUD, THUD, THUD pounds with fury above her head.

> DOROTHY
> Clem!

In her frenzy to open the door, she drops the LAMP, and it SHATTERS. The flame catches on the carpet.

Dorothy tries to stomp it out, but her efforts aren't very effective.

She pounds on the door.

> DOROTHY (CONT'D)
> Help! Clem! Help!

INT. BERGMAN MANOR - CLEM'S ROOM - SAME

Clem hears the THUD, THUD, THUD and Dorothy's muffled voice. He jumps out of bed, and sways a bit from the head wound. He stumbles out the door.

INT. BERGMAN MANOR - HALLWAY - SAME

It's very dark.

Clem starts down the hallway, but someone grabs him from behind.

Clem jams his elbow backwards, once, twice, three times, and his attacker finally disengages.

Dorothy's scream keeps Clem from following up with his attacker. He stumbles down the hallway.

INT. BERGMAN MANOR - ODIN'S OFFICE - SAME

Dorothy is still trying to stomp out the flames, but they're growing.

Clem BURSTS through the DOOR.

He rips the drapes from the window and uses them to stifle the flames.

Dorothy throws the naked windows open and sucks in the
fresh air. Moonlight streams in -- now the only light.

                         CLEM
           Are you all right? What happened?

Dorothy flings herself into his arms.

                         DOROTHY
           I've never been so scared. The
           door locked, and I couldn't get
           out. I thought you... I thought --

She buries her face in Clem's shoulder to keep from
getting hysterical. Clem strokes her back.

                         CLEM
           I'm safe. We're both safe.

Clem sways again, and his weight sags against Dorothy.

                         DOROTHY
           Clem, your head.

Clem touches the bandage. It's wet with fresh blood.
Dorothy helps him to a chair.

                         CLEM
           Someone attacked me in the
           hallway.

                         DOROTHY
           Clem, you need to get away from
           here... away from me... as fast as
           you can.

                         CLEM
           I can't. Not yet.

Lights turn on in the foyer, and Odin comes in, followed
shortly by Dr. Campbell, Arthur, and Samuel. Odin flips
the lights on.

                         ODIN
           What's going on in here?

                         ARTHUR
           We heard shouts for help.

Dr. Campbell goes to Clem and unwraps his head bandage to
inspect his wound.

Dorothy searches for words to explain, and Clem comes to
the rescue:

                              CLEM
          It's my fault entirely. I couldn't
          sleep and came to find something
          to read. I suppose I took a wrong
          turn, thought this was the
          library. Head wound, you know.
          Dorothy heard me and thought I was
          a burglar. She surprised me, and I
          dropped the lamp. I'm afraid I
          ruined your curtains trying to put
          out the fire. My sincere
          apologies. I'll pay for the
          damages, of course.

                              ARTHUR
          I'm just glad no one's dead. I
          don't think my wife could handle
          another body popping up.

                              SAMUEL
          Mine either.

                              DR. CAMPBELL
          I'll need to redress this. Let's
          get you up to your room.

INT. BERGMAN MANOR - FOYER - LATER

Samuel and Arthur help a woozy Clem up the stairs, Dr.
Campbell following just behind them.

Dorothy starts after them, but Odin grabs her arm and
holds her back. He waits until the men have reached the
top and disappeared.

                              ODIN
          A wrong turn to the library?
          Really?

                              DOROTHY
          Why else would he be in your
          office?

They're locked in a stare-down for a moment. Finally,
Odin releases her arm, almost flinging her away.

                              ODIN
          Get to bed. You've got a lot to do
          tomorrow.

INT. BERGMAN MANOR - ODIN'S OFFICE - MOMENTS LATER

Odin enters and is about to turn out the lights, but at
his feet, he notices the forgotten journals. He picks
them up and inspects the bindings, which are blank. He
shrugs and throws them on a nearby table. Lights out.

INT. BERGMAN MANOR - CLEM'S ROOM - SAME

Arthur and Samuel deposit Clem on the bed. Dr. Campbell
supervises until they leave.

>   DR. CAMPBELL
>   Take my advice, son. If you don't
>   want trouble, leave the girl be.

>   CLEM
>   Who's going to give me trouble?

>   DR. CAMPBELL
>   The girl. Fate. Ghosts. Bad luck.
>   Call it what you want, fellas she
>   runs around with always seem to
>   run into trouble.

>   CLEM
>   Odin?

Dr. Campbell almost laughs.

>   DR. CAMPBELL
>   I've known Odin since he was a
>   boy. He's a bit rough around the
>   edges, sure, but I don't believe
>   he would hurt anybody. Besides,
>   he's too much a man of business,
>   just like his father. He'd sooner
>   get rid of the maid than paying
>   customers.

>   CLEM
>   Then why doesn't he? If she's such
>   bad luck for paying customers, why
>   doesn't he fire her?

The conversation is making Dr. Campbell uncomfortable.

>   DR. CAMPBELL
>   Get some rest.

He leaves.

Clem waits until Dr. Campbell's FOOTSTEPS FADE before getting up to lock the door. He takes the desk chair and shoves it under his door handle for good measure.

INT. BERGMAN MANOR - CLEM'S ROOM - DAY

Clem finishes dressing, pulling on his jacket. His hand is on the knob when he stops and turns around. He goes to the desk, opens the drawer, and stuffs his journal with all its newspaper clippings and the old photograph in the inside pocket of his jacket.

INT. BERGMAN MANOR - FOYER - MOMENTS LATER

Clem reaches the bottom of the stairs and looks around. Pokes his head in the library. Wanders down the hall toward Odin's office and comes back a moment later. Goes into the dining hall.

INT. BERGMAN MANOR - DINING HALL - SAME

It's empty here too. Clem goes through to the kitchen.

INT. BERGMAN MANOR - KITCHEN - SAME

Mrs. O'Toole slaves away over the stove. She looks up when Clem comes in.

                    MRS. O'TOOLE
          Another bicarbonate of soda?

                    CLEM
          No, thank you. Where is everyone?

                    MRS. O'TOOLE
          The whole lot of them decided to
          have a beach day.

                    CLEM
          Do you know where Dorothy is?

                    MRS. O'TOOLE
          I probably oughtn't to tell you,
          but... all the way upstairs.
          Cleaning the storage.

                    CLEM
          Thank you.

He leaves.

INT. BERGMAN MANOR - UPPER FLOOR - DAY

Dorothy shakes out a furniture cover. Dust flies
everywhere, making her cough.

Clem appears in the doorway.

                    DOROTHY
          Aren't you supposed to be resting?

                    CLEM
          I needed to see you. See that
          you're okay after last night.

                    DOROTHY
          Odin knows we lied.

                    CLEM
          Well. It wasn't one of my best,
          but it's all I could come up with
          on the spot.

Clem roams through the room, taking in old pictures,
books, everything.

                    DOROTHY
          Well now you know I'm all right.
          You should leave.

                    CLEM
          This from the girl who wanted to
          stay in my room last night.

                    DOROTHY
          Clem. Don't you see how serious
          this is? We both almost died last
          night. And I'm this close to
          getting fired.

His eyes catch something on the ceiling.

                    CLEM
          What's up there?

Dorothy follows his gaze.

Barely noticeable, in the corner, there's a hatch in the
ceiling.

                    DOROTHY
          Give it up, Clem. Go home.

Clem's finally had it.

                              CLEM
          Go home? To what? I have nothing.
          No one. Not even a place to live.
          The only family I had came here
          and died, and I want to know why.
          And I'm not leaving until I do.

                           DOROTHY
          Or you'll die finding the answer,
          just like your uncle did.

                            CLEM
          So be it.

He jumps and pulls on the latch, and the hatch opens.
Something CRASHES to the floor, kicking up a cloud of
dust.

Dorothy and Clem choke and cough. Clem waves away the
dust. When it clears, he looks at the thing on the floor.

It's a large bundle of canvas.

Clem bends to unwrap it. As he folds it back, they can
see that it's covered in blood stains.

Dorothy covers her mouth in horror.

A gold locket tumbles out of its folds. Clem picks it up.
The initials on the front read: "A.B."

                        CLEM (CONT'D)
          Agnes Bergman.

Clem looks down at the blood-stained canvas and back up
at Dorothy.

                        CLEM (CONT'D)
          Still think she committed suicide?

Dorothy shakes her head.

Clem releases a small clasp on the locket, and it pops
open. Inside is a picture of Agnes holding a baby.

                        CLEM (CONT'D)
          Hello. What's this?

Dorothy looks over his shoulder.

                           DOROTHY
          We have to get those journals.

INT. BERGMAN MANOR - ODIN'S OFFICE - MOMENTS LATER

Dorothy and Clem sneak inside and shut the door softly.

Dorothy goes straight to the shelf with the journals, but the last two are missing.

>   DOROTHY
>   They're not here.

>   CLEM
>   They must be.

He goes to help her search the shelf. They pull out several journals, check the dates, and put them back.

Dorothy finally spots them on the table where Odin left them.

>   DOROTHY
>   There.

Clem's hand is just touching the leather binding when the door opens, and Odin enters.

Fury is all over his face. Clem steps in front of Dorothy.

>   ODIN
>   Thieves! Get out!

He grabs Clem by the lapel and shoves him out the door. He grabs Dorothy by the arm and drags her out too.

INT. BERGMAN MANOR - FOYER - SAME

With Clem's lapel in one fist and Dorothy's arm in the other, Odin storms toward the front door.

>   DOROTHY
>   Odin, you don't understand.

>   CLEM
>   It's not what you think.

EXT. BERGMAN MANOR - FRONT DOOR - SAME

Odin flings Dorothy first, and she stumbles to her knees on the gravel drive. Then with both hands, he tosses Clem after her.

                         ODIN
          I never want to see either of you
          around here again.

                         DOROTHY
          But --

                         ODIN
          Get out!

His fury terrifies her, and she cowers on the ground.

He storms back inside without another word.

Clem helps Dorothy up and wipes the gravel from her hands
and dress.

                         CLEM
          I'm sorry.

Without a word, but on the verge of tears, Dorothy turns
and walks down the gravel drive away from the Manor.

Clem casts a last glance at the hulking Manor before
following her.

INT. BERGMAN MANOR - CLEM'S ROOM - SAME

Odin flings open the door and pulls Clem's suitcase out
of the closet. He opens drawers and shoves clothes into
the suitcase.

Dr. Campbell stops in the open doorway, one hand behind
his back.

                         DR. CAMPBELL
          I thought I might check on young
          Mr. Beauregard. What's going on?

                         ODIN
          Bastard was trying to steal from
          me. I knew it. I knew it last
          night. And she was helping him.

                         DR. CAMPBELL
          Who?

                         ODIN
          I'll have to apologize for the
          service over the next few days,
          Benjamin. It'll be hard without
          Dorothy.

Dr. Campbell's eyes flash. He steps inside and closes the door behind him.

> DR. CAMPBELL
> Where is Dorothy, Odin?

> ODIN
> I fired her. Threw her out. Little vixen.

> DR. CAMPBELL
> You threw out your own niece --

Odin freezes. Something like realization crosses his face, and then fear.

By the time Odin turns, Dr. Campbell has raised his hand from behind his back, a hand that's holding a syringe. He plunges it into Odin's neck, and the giant of a man falls in a heap to the floor.

INT. TRAIN STATION - SUNSET

Dorothy sits on a bench looking dejected.

Clem chats on the phone in a booth on the far wall. The conversation ends, and he pushes the folding door open.

Clem takes a seat next to Dorothy.

> CLEM
> My uncle's secretary is going to wire us some money for the train tickets. I think you'll like the city. There's a lot of hot spots, good music, juice joints if you know where to find them. And I can ask Jane -- that's my uncle's secretary -- I can ask her if she'll take a roommate until --

> DOROTHY
> I know how you feel now. About your uncle. Odin's the closest thing to family I've ever known.

> CLEM
> I'm sorry. Truly.

She reaches into a pocket and produces the two journals.

Clem takes them from her.

                    DOROTHY
          I figured as long as we were
          getting thrown out as thieves...

Clem gives Dorothy's hand a squeeze and kisses her on the
temple. She scoots a little closer to read over his
shoulder.

He opens one of them to a random page and reads aloud.

                    CLEM
          "May 3, 1905. Agnes went into
          labor during the evening meal.
          It's now been three hours. The
          doctor says it will be awhile yet.
          It may be tomorrow before the
          child is born. I've sent for Odin,
          but I don't know if he will come.
          Agnes does not want him to come or
          even know of the child's
          existence. She says she can't bear
          her brother to know of her
          disgrace."

He flips to an entry a few pages ahead. He doesn't seem
to notice Dorothy pulling away, realization dawning on
her face.

                    CLEM (CONT'D)
          "May 10. The Baptism was today. We
          had a hard time convincing the
          pastor to baptize a child born out
          of wedlock, but I think my
          worsening health gave him a soft
          heart. My granddaughter has been
          christened Dorothy Francis
          Bergman..."

His voices trails off. He looks at Dorothy, but she
stares straight ahead.

                    DOROTHY
          I'm the baby in Agnes's locket.

They sit in silence, absorbing this revelation.

Finally, Dorothy grabs the book from Clem. A folded piece
of paper slides out from the back cover in the exchange,
but Dorothy doesn't notice. As Clem bends to pick up the
fallen paper, Dorothy flips through the journal's pages.

                    DOROTHY (CONT'D)
          It must say who my father is
          somewhere. It must.

Clem unfolds the paper and scans its contents.

                    CLEM
          Jeepers.

                    DOROTHY
          Look, after Franz died, someone
          else continued to write in here.
          It must be Agnes, listen to this.
          "The only thing worse than facing
          Odin's disappointment is the
          thought of facing Benjamin again.
          He and his wife arrive next week."

She keeps flipping through pages, but she reaches the
end.

                    DOROTHY (CONT'D)
          This is the last entry. "Benjamin
          refuses to acknowledge Dorothy as
          his own. He ignores me completely.
          I think he may be preying on the
          new maid. This can't go on."

Clem's eyes haven't left the letter in his hand. He
reads.

                    CLEM
          "My Dearest Brother. How I wish I
          could find the words to express my
          regret for all the shame and
          sorrow I've caused you. Father
          found it in his heart to forgive
          me before his passing, and I hope
          someday you'll find forgiveness in
          your heart as well. I beg you not
          only to forgive me for my past
          sins, but also for the one I am
          about to commit. I see no other
          way forward, no other way to rid
          the world of this miserable
          creature."

Dorothy finally looks up.

                    CLEM (CONT'D)
          "I leave my precious daughter in
          your care. Please take care of
          Dorothy as if she were your own.
          You will be the only family she
          has left, truly. And please, never
          tell her of her mother's shame.
          Goodbye, my dear brother.
                    (MORE)

                    CLEM (CONT'D)
God be with you always. Your
loving sister, Agnes."

                    DOROTHY
Her suicide note.

                    CLEM
"For the sin I am about to commit.
I see no other way to rid the
world of this miserable creature.
You will be the only family she
has left, truly." This isn't a
suicide note.

                    DOROTHY
Sounds like one to me.

                    CLEM
She was going to kill <u>him</u>. Your
father. But he must have gotten to
her first. That would explain the
blood stains and the locket. He
killed her and then made it look
like she killed herself. And the
"B" on the cuff links. It stands
for Benjamin, not Bergman. Don't
you see?

Dorothy absorbs this information. And other pieces start
to come together. The realization is horrible.

                    DOROTHY
Clem. Dr. Campbell's first name is
Benjamin.

INT. BERGMAN MANOR - HALLWAY - EVENING

Dr. Campbell walks down the hallway and stops at Clem's
door. He puts a hand to the knob, but the appearance of
the Price sisters stops him.

                    IRMA
Oh, Dr. Campbell. Are you going to
check on Clem? How is the poor
dear?

                    DR. CAMPBELL
He's still resting.

                    EILEEN
You missed quite the brawl on the
beach, Doc. Shame.

He smiles as they pass him. He waits until they are out of sight before he enters Clem's room.

INT. TRAIN STATION - EVENING

Clem snaps up the letter and the journals and stuffs them inside his jacket pocket. He grabs Dorothy's hand and leads her toward the door. Dorothy pulls away.

>   DOROTHY
>   What are you doing?

>   CLEM
>   We have to go back.

>   DOROTHY
>   What? I'm not going back there.
>   Why would I go back?

>   CLEM
>   Dr. Campbell is a murderer,
>   Dorothy. He murdered your mother.
>   He murdered Thomas. He murdered my
>   uncle. Look.

He pulls out the old photograph.

>   CLEM (CONT'D)
>   That boy. It's my uncle. He was at
>   Bergman Manor the same summer your
>   mother died, I'm sure of it. Maybe
>   he even saw what happened to her.
>   And look.

He pulls out the old newspaper articles and sorts through them, discarding the irrelevant ones on the floor.

>   CLEM (CONT'D)
>   Look. The man who died at the
>   beginning of this summer. Look at
>   the article. Dr. Campbell is in
>   the picture in the background
>   there. Do you see?

Sure enough, in the picture, Dr. Campbell is among the onlookers.

>   CLEM (CONT'D)
>   Monty recognized him. That's why
>   he came back. He knew what
>   Campbell did, and Campbell killed
>   him for it.

                         DOROTHY
               If all that is true, Clem, why
               should we go back? So he can kill
               us too? Let's just call the
               sheriff.

                         CLEM
               Yes. Let's call the Lincoln County
               Sheriff's Department. The ones who
               investigated six deaths and
               couldn't figure out that a single
               one of them was murder. I'm sure
               they'll believe us though. We have
               rock solid evidence. Murder
               weapons. Fingerprints.
               Eyewitnesses.

                         DOROTHY
               Okay. I get it. But if we go back,
               what then? We tell Dr. Campbell we
               know what he's done and hope he
               turns himself in?

                         CLEM
               We tell Odin. We gather more
               evidence.

Dorothy really doesn't want to do this. But finally, she
nods in agreement, and they walk out of the station.

INT. BERGMAN MANOR - CLEM'S ROOM - NIGHT

Dr. Campbell takes a tie from Clem's suitcase, still
sitting on the bed half-packed. He wraps it around each
hand a couple times, pulling it taut.

He bends toward Odin's still unconscious body.

EXT. BERGMAN MANOR - SAME

A cab pulls into the drive, and Clem and Dorothy climb
out. Dorothy puts a hand on Clem's arm as he pays the
fare.

                         DOROTHY
               Do you hear that?

Clem listens. Sure enough. From somewhere inside, THUD,
THUD, THUD.

                         CLEM
               Something's wrong.

They fly up the front steps. Clem reaches the door first
and yanks, but it's locked. He rattles it back and forth,
but it's no good.

                    CLEM (CONT'D)
          We have to find another way in.

                    DOROTHY
          The back door will be locked too.

                    CLEM
          Come on.

He runs back down the steps and over a flowerbed to the
library windows. Dorothy follows.

The THUD, THUD, THUD GROWS in VOLUME and INTENSITY.

Clem looks around and spots a line of paving stones. He
kicks one until it comes loose from the surrounding dirt.
He picks it up.

                    CLEM (CONT'D)
          Stand back.

He uses it to BREAK one of the bay seat WINDOWS.

INT. BERGMAN MANOR - CLEM'S ROOM - SAME

Dr. Campbell hears the SHATTERING GLASS and looks up.

EXT. BERGMAN MANOR - SAME

Clem reaches gingerly through to unlock the window and
pull it open. The THUD, THUD, THUD comes to a SUDDEN
STOP.

Clem and Dorothy look at one another, wondering if that's
a good sign or a bad one.

                    CLEM
          Come on. Careful of the broken
          glass.

Clem gives Dorothy a boost through the window.

INT. BERGMAN MANOR - LIBRARY - SAME

Dorothy scrambles inside and turns to help Clem climb in
behind her.

The lights come on, and they both whirl around.

Arthur and Samuel stand in the doorway.

                    ARTHUR
          What's going on here?

Dr. Campbell rushes up behind Arthur.

                    DR. CAMPBELL
          Stop them!

                    CLEM
          What?

                    DR. CAMPBELL
          Don't let them get away! They're
          thieves and murderers.

                    DOROTHY
          No!

                    DR. CAMPBELL
          I just discovered Odin's body in
          his room. He's dead.

Dorothy cries out.

                    CLEM
          You bastard!

But Arthur and Samuel need no more explanation. They run
at Clem and tackle him to the ground.

                    DOROTHY
          Clem!

Dorothy lunges toward the fray, but Dr. Campbell wraps
her up from behind.

                    CLEM
          It's him! Stop! It wasn't me!

Samuel slugs Clem in the jaw, stunning him. Clem
struggles to remain conscious.

                    DR. CAMPBELL
          Tie his hands.

Arthur grabs a cord from the drapes and uses it to bind
Clem's hands.

                         DOROTHY
            Stop! Arthur! Don't trust him!
            Clem's not the murderer! It's --

                         DR. CAMPBELL
            Shut up!

Dr. Campbell covers her mouth with his hand. She bites
him, and he whips her around and smacks her across the
face. She falls to her knees. Campbell immediately looks
remorseful.

                         CLEM
                  (weakly)
            Dorothy...

Arthur and Samuel watch with wide eyes.

                         DR. CAMPBELL
            Samuel, Arthur, take Mr.
            Beauregard to the cellar and lock
            him in there until the police
            arrive. I'll look after Dorothy
            and call the police myself.

Samuel and Arthur look unsure, but they each take one of
Clem's arms and drag him to his feet.

Dr. Campbell watches them drag Clem from the room.

                         DOROTHY
            Clem!

Dorothy tries to follow, but Dr. Campbell wraps her up
again.

                         DOROTHY (CONT'D)
            Clem! Let me go! Clem!

Dr. Campbell holds her tight. He whispers in her ear.

                         DR. CAMPBELL
            Listen to me, Dorothy. Listen very
            carefully. If you calm down,
            everything will be just fine. But
            if you continue to scream, I will
            have no choice but to kill your
            precious Mr. Beauregard.

                         DOROTHY
            Like you killed my mother?

                         DR. CAMPBELL
          That was self-defense, Dorothy.
          She tried to kill me. I never
          meant to hurt her.

                         IRMA (O.S.)
          Odin? Arthur?

INT. BERGMAN MANOR - STAIRS - SAME

Irma stands at the top of the stairs with all the other
women gathered behind her. They all clutch their robes
shut over their nightgowns. Irma yells over the
bannister.

                         IRMA
          We heard screams! Is everyone all
          right?

INT. BERGMAN MANOR - LIBRARY - SAME

Dr. Campbell grits his teeth.

                         DR. CAMPBELL
          Everything's just fine, Miss
          Price! Go back to bed!

INT. BERGMAN MANOR - STAIRS - SAME

The women all exchange looks with one another and shrug.
Nora, Lillian, and the Guillaumes turn to go back to
their rooms. But the Price sisters remain.

INT. BERGMAN MANOR - CELLAR - SAME

Arthur and Samuel lead Clem through a dark corridor of
wine racks toward a sturdy-looking door at the very end.

Clem shakes his head, trying to clear the haze and regain
full control. He struggles against his captors.

                         CLEM
          Don't do this, fellas. Dr.
          Campbell is the real murderer.
          He's dangerous. Please.

                         ARTHUR
          You think we're stupid enough to
          buy that after we found you in
          Odin's office last night?

Clem struggles more, but he's still too weak. Suddenly, desperately:

                    CLEM
          Agnes! Help me, Agnes! Help!
          Agnes!

                    SAMUEL
          Who the hell is Agnes?

But everything starts to RATTLE and SHAKE. WINE BOTTLES CLINK on their racks. SOFTLY AT FIRST but GROWING IN VIOLENCE.

Suddenly, a CORK POPS and whizzes past Samuel's head. Then ANOTHER POP, and a cork hits Arthur in the shoulder.

                    ARTHUR
          What the hell?

The BOTTLES SHAKE SO VIOLENTLY, they begin to SHATTER. CORKS POP and WHIZ EVERYWHERE.

Arthur drops Clem first and bolts. It takes a cork to the face to make Samuel follow suit.

Clem crumples to his knees.

Suddenly, the CHAOS STOPS, leaving wine spilled and pooling around shards of glass and corks.

Clem stretches and contorts his body to grab a shard of glass nearby. He maneuvers it in his hand to cut away at the cord around his wrists. His hand starts to bleed, but he keeps cutting until the cord gives way.

Clem staggers to his feet and runs.

INT. BERGMAN MANOR - FOYER - SAME

Clem reaches the foyer to find Irma and Eileen crouched over a barely conscious Dorothy, who's holding a hand to her bleeding head.

                    CLEM
          What happened?

                    EILEEN
          It was Dr. Campbell, Clem. He had
          poor Dorothy all wrapped up, and
          when he saw us coming down the
          stairs --

                              IRMA
              He threw Dorothy into the
              bannister, and she hit her head.

                              EILEEN
              And then he just bolted out the
              front door.

                              IRMA
              What's going on, Clem?

                              CLEM
              Don't leave her alone.

Clem runs toward the front door. Over his shoulder:

                              CLEM (CONT'D)
              And call the police.

EXT. BERGMAN MANOR - SAME

Clem comes out on the front steps, but it's dark. Dr.
Campbell is nowhere in sight.

A SCRAPING comes from the direction of the garage, and
Clem can just make out a door being pushed open.

Clem takes off in that direction.

                              CLEM
              Campbell! Stop!

Headlights flash on just as Clem arrives at the open
door.

The ENGINE REVS, and the car lurches forward. Clem has to
jump on the hood to keep from being hit. As the car
emerges, the moonlight reveals that it's a convertible
with the top down.

The car breaks so suddenly that Clem goes flying. The car
moves again, threatening to run Clem over.

He rolls away just in time and springs to his feet.

He runs and jumps onto the running board.

Dr. Campbell swerves as Clem lunges for him, causing Clem
to topple inside.

Clem regains his balance and punches Dr. Campbell in the
face.

The car takes a sharp turn off the drive and CRASHES into a tree.

Dr. Campbell opens the door and topples out. Clem crawls after him.

Dr. Campbell makes a run for it, but Clem tackles him from behind. Dr. Campbell rolls onto his back and socks Clem in the nose.

Dr. Campbell shoves Clem to the ground and gets on top of him. His fingers wrap around Clem's throat.

Clem struggles to tear Dr. Campbell's hands away and chokes on the blood streaming from his nose.

Suddenly, there's a LOUD, BONE-CRUNCHING THWACK, and Dr. Campbell falls forward limply, smothering Clem.

Clem rolls Dr. Campbell off his chest.

Dorothy stands over them with a fire poker.

INT. BERGMAN MANOR - DINING HALL - EARLY MORNING

Clem sits at the head of the table. On either side of him stand two uniformed sheriff's deputies.

Detective Gates comes through the door. Before it shuts, Clem can see all the other guests in the foyer huddled in twos and threes. A couple of them speak with uniformed deputies, apparently giving statements.

>   DETECTIVE GATES
>   Mr. Beauregard.

>   CLEM
>   Detective.

Gates takes the chair on Clem's left.

>   DETECTIVE GATES
>   Looks like you managed to make
>   quite a mess of Bergman Manor.

Clem looks away, not wanting to confirm or deny anything.

>   CLEM
>   Where's Dorothy?

>   DETECTIVE GATES
>   The maid?

                    CLEM
          The owner of Bergman Manor.

Detective Gates raises his eyebrows.

                    DETECTIVE GATES
          Not so fast, Mr. Beauregard.
          Odin's in bad shape all right, but
          he's not dead yet.

                    CLEM
          He's not. Thank God!

Gates frowns -- he's supposed to be getting information
from Clem, not the other way around.

                    DETECTIVE GATES
          You lied to me. You told me you
          didn't know what your uncle was
          working on here.

                    CLEM
          I did not lie. When you asked me,
          I didn't know.

                    DETECTIVE GATES
          Then why did you come here?

                    CLEM
          It's what we P-I's call a hunch.

                    DETECTIVE GATES
          Dr. Campbell says you and the maid
          stole from Mr. Bergman and tried
          to kill him, and when he caught
          you, you attacked him too.

                    CLEM
          He's right.

Clem pulls Franz's journals out of his pocket and sets
them on the table in front of Gates.

                    CLEM (CONT'D)
          About the stealing. I took these
          from Odin's office without his
          knowledge or permission.
          Everything else is a lie.

                    DETECTIVE GATES
          Then why don't you tell me what
          really happened?

                         CLEM
          Dr. Campbell is a murderer.

Clem pulls out his notebook and sets it on the table next
to Franz's journals.

                         CLEM (CONT'D)
          It's all in there.

EXT. BERGMAN MANOR - SAME

Dorothy paces up and down the drive, now filled with
police cars and an ambulance. A sheriff's deputy nearby
keeps his eyes trained on Dorothy.

Out of the house comes Odin on a stretcher. Dorothy
rushes over to him and takes his hand.

                         DOROTHY
               Odin.

His neck is bruised where Dr. Campbell tried to strangle
him. He tries to form words, but he has no voice.

                         DOROTHY (CONT'D)
          Don't try to speak. I'm here.
          You're going to be fine.
          Everything's going to be fine.
          I'll look after the Manor until
          you return. Don't you worry about
          a thing.

Odin reaches up and touches Dorothy's cheek.

They reach the ambulance, and Dorothy is forced to let go
of Odin's hand as the medical crew lifts the stretcher
inside. The doors shut.

The ambulance drives away.

Dorothy turns back toward the house.

Clem stands in the doorway. He starts down the steps.

Dorothy runs to him and throws her arms around his neck.
He wraps his arms around her and holds her close.

A DEPUTY comes out the door.

                         DEPUTY
          Miss Francis? Detective Gates
          would like to see you.

INT. BERGMAN MANOR - FOYER - SAME

Gates meets Dorothy and Clem as they enter.

                    DETECTIVE GATES
          He says he'll tell us everything
          we want to know, but only if he
          gets to talk to you first.

                    DOROTHY
          What could he possibly want to say
          to me that I would want to hear?

Gates shrugs.

                    DETECTIVE GATES
          You don't have to, of course, but
          it would sure make my job a
          helluva lot easier.

Dorothy looks to Clem as if asking for his input.

                    CLEM
          I'll go with you if you want.

                    DETECTIVE GATES
          He asked for Dorothy. Alone.

Dorothy takes a moment to think before deciding.

                    DOROTHY
          Okay. I'll see him.

INT. BERGMAN MANOR - ODIN'S OFFICE - SAME

Dr. Campbell sits handcuffed in the guest chair. A deputy
stands guard a few feet away.

The door opens, and Gates ushers Dorothy in.

                    DETECTIVE GATES
          Here she is, Campbell. Spill.

                    DR. CAMPBELL
          I'd like a moment alone with her,
          if you please.

                    DOROTHY
          It's okay, Detective. I'm not
          afraid of him.

Dr. Campbell smiles.

Gates and the deputy head out the door. Just before it
shuts:

> DETECTIVE GATES
> Holler if he even looks like he's
> going to make trouble. We'll be
> right outside the door.

Dorothy nods, and the door shuts. She moves to the far
side of the room, keeping as much distance and furniture
between them as possible.

> DOROTHY
> What do you want?

> DR. CAMPBELL
> To tell you I'm sorry.

> DOROTHY
> About which part?

> DR. CAMPBELL
> For that wound on your head. And
> for hitting you. Truly, I never
> wanted... I never want to hurt
> you.

> DOROTHY
> Anything else?

> DR. CAMPBELL
> Yes. I'm sorry about your mother.
> About Agnes. I've spent the last
> twenty years trying to make up for
> what I did to her.

> DOROTHY
> How could you possibly do that?

> DR. CAMPBELL
> By watching over you. Protecting
> you. Making sure no man ever
> treated you the way I treated her.

Dorothy stares at him in horror.

> DOROTHY
> You're a lunatic.

> DR. CAMPBELL
> Dorothy. My beautiful daughter.
> Can you ever forgive me?

EXT. BEACH - DAY

Clem stands on the beach studying the old photograph of
12-year-old Monty.

Irma comes down the pathway behind him and comes to stand
next to him.

                    IRMA
          What have you got there?

                    CLEM
          A picture of my uncle when he was
          a boy. Only, you know something? I
          don't know who the woman is
          standing next to him.

Irma looks at the picture.

                    IRMA
          Why, that's old Gloria Montgomery.
          I think it is anyway. She's
          younger there. She passed away the
          summer after Eileen and I started
          coming here. Ten years ago. Or is
          it eleven now?

                    CLEM
          Great-grandmother Gloria. I never
          met her.

They fall into thoughtful silence for a moment.

                    IRMA
          I thought you might want to know
          they've finally taken the good
          doctor away.

                    CLEM
          And the other guests?

                    IRMA
          Packing to leave. Arthur and
          Samuel feel like fools, as they
          should. I guess maybe all of us
          should. Except you. How did you
          know about Dr. Campbell?

Clem laughs to himself.

                    CLEM
          Would you think I was crazy if I
          told you Agnes Bergman helped me
          figure it out?

                    IRMA
          Clem, dear, you should know by now
          that if anyone would believe that
          story, it would be me and Eileen.

Clem smiles, and Irma smiles back.

INT. BERGMAN MANOR - FOYER - SAME

Dorothy sits on the bottom step of the stairs, resting
her head on the bannister.

Eileen comes from behind her down the stairs.

                    EILEEN
          Darling, you look positively
          bushed.

Dorothy sits up straight, and Eileen takes a seat next to
her. Eileen takes her hand, which surprises Dorothy.

                    EILEEN (CONT'D)
          I know. Irma and I have not been
          the models of kindness towards
          you, and I apologize for that.

                    DOROTHY
          Don't mention it.

                    EILEEN
          And I hope it isn't presumptuous.
          But Irma and I talked it over. We
          would like to stay and help you
          get Bergman Manor back on its
          feet. Perhaps if people see that
          not all the guests have left...

Dorothy breaks down. Eileen puts an arm around her and
pulls her close. Like a mother would.

                    EILEEN (CONT'D)
          That's it, dear. You cry just as
          much as you need to.

Clem and Irma come through the front door.

                    EILEEN (CONT'D)
          Look, honey. Your very own knight
          in shining armor.

Dorothy straightens and wipes her eyes.

Eileen stands, and she and Irma head up the stairs. Clem takes her vacated spot next to Dorothy.

Dorothy searches her pockets for a handkerchief, but Clem beats her to it. He holds one out for her. She accepts it and blows her nose.

> DOROTHY
> I'm sorry. I'm just... just...

> CLEM
> I know.

Clem holds up a freshly picked flower. Dorothy takes it.

> DOROTHY
> Is this a farewell flower?

> CLEM
> No. That is an I'm-in-love-with-you-but-this-isn't-the-right-time-to-tell-you-so flower.

Dorothy smiles as she lifts the flower to her nose, but she soon turns serious again.

> DOROTHY
> He asked me to forgive him.

> CLEM
> Did you?

> DOROTHY
> I told him I didn't know how, but I hoped that someday I could.

> CLEM
> That's more generous than I would have been.

> DOROTHY
> Agnes couldn't or wouldn't forgive, and it destroyed them both.

Clem concedes.

After a moment, Clem clears his throat and changes the subject.

> CLEM
> Dorothy, I know I've got nothing to offer. The truth is, up until now, I've been sort of a cad.
> (MORE)

                    CLEM (CONT'D)
          All play and no work.
          Irresponsible. Broke. Homeless.
          But if I go back to the city, work
          hard, make something of myself...

Dorothy turns and pulls Clem toward her and kisses him.

                    CLEM (CONT'D)
          Is that a yes?

                    DOROTHY
          You never asked a question.

                    CLEM
          But you know what I want to ask.
          Don't you?

                    DOROTHY
          I promised Odin I would look after
          Bergman Manor until he's well.

                    CLEM
          But when he is well?

                    DOROTHY
          You'll be the first to know.

Clem smiles and they kiss again.

INT. MONTGOMERY'S OFFICE - DAY

Clem sits behind Monty's desk with his feet up, pipe
hanging from his mouth, reading a newspaper with the
headline: "LOCAL P.I. SOLVES BERGMAN MANOR MURDERS."

Jane comes in the door and slaps a pile of newspapers on
the desk, all carrying headlines for the same story.

                    JANE
          The phone's been ringing off the
          hook. Everyone wants the private
          investigator who solved the
          Bergman Manor murders to solve
          their cases too. With this many
          clients, you'll be able to give me
          that raise Monty was always
          promising.

Clem folds his newspaper and tosses it on top of the
others.

                         CLEM
          Sure, but will it be enough to get
          a nice place and support a family?

                         JANE
          I never thought I'd see the day.
          She must be a real knockout.

Clem smiles.

                         CLEM
          You can judge for yourself. She'll
          be here any minute.

                         JANE
          But I thought --

                         CLEM
          Her uncle was allowed to go home
          last night, and Dorothy tells me
          the Price sisters have proven to
          be quite helpful.

                         DOROTHY (O.S.)
          Hello?

Clem and Jane go to the door.

INT. OFFICE - SAME

Having traded her maid's dress for something stylish and
delectable, Dorothy IS a real knockout.

Clem can't help himself. He stares.

Dorothy becomes self-conscious. She touches her hat, her
necklace, her dress.

                         DOROTHY
          Is something wrong? Am I not
          wearing it right?

                         JANE
          You're perfect, dear. You must be
          Dorothy.

                         DOROTHY
          And you must be Jane.

They shake hands.

                         DOROTHY (CONT'D)
          Clem?

Clem finally shakes himself back to functionality.

>   CLEM
>   Yeah. Dorothy, this is Jane
>   Miller, my uncle's -- that is, my
>   secretary. Jane, this is Dorothy
>   Francis Bergman.

The women giggle. Clem doesn't get it.

>   DOROTHY
>   Come on, Detective. Take me to
>   lunch.

Clem smiles and grabs his hat. Dorothy loops her arm through his, and they walk out the door.

A painter is just painting the last new letter on the door. It now reads:

"CLEMENT BEAUREGARD

PRIVATE INVESTIGATOR"

>   FADE OUT.

THE END

WRITER'S NOTE

I'm greatly inspired by classic films, especially ones made during the Golden Age of Hollywood. In my wildest dreams, filmmaking returns to that Golden Age, and producers are falling over themselves to buy scripts like mine. Until then, publishing my screenplays as books will suffice. The important thing is that this story is now out in the world for people to enjoy instead of collecting cyber-dust in my computer files.

Truthfully, I'm a little embarrassed by how long "Bergman Manor" did just that. I finished the first draft of this script almost seven years ago, completely reworked it shortly after that, and have revisited it every year or so since then. I'd thought about publishing this and other screenplays long ago, but it took a pandemic and a stay-at-home order to motivate me to actually do it.

If you enjoyed "Bergman Manor," stick around. I hope to have my next script in your hands very soon.

Many blessings to you and yours!

ACKNOWLEDGMENTS

I have to start by thanking the person who gave me the idea and impetus to write this particular story: Andrea Lynch. Although the final version turned out quite different from the "Bergman Manor" of our initial conversations, it was her encouragement and enthusiasm at the beginning that got me through that all-important first draft. Andrea, I hope you like the way it turned out.

Many thanks to three people who taught me everything I know about writing and storytelling: Caryn Collette, Susan Odenbaugh, and Christopher Riley. I can't overstate the impact you three have had on my life.

Without Morgan Gist MacDonald, this script would still be collecting cyber-dust. Thank you, Morgan, for your friendship and your advice.

Thank you, also, to all the family members, friends, and colleagues who have read my scripts, given me notes, and cheered me on over the years. Your generosity and love humble me.

Above all, I must give all thanks and praise to Christ, my Divine Spouse. I am nothing without Him: "Whom have I in heaven but Thee? And there is nothing upon earth that I desire besides Thee. My flesh and my heart may fail, but God is the strength of my heart and my portion for ever" (Ps 73:25-26).

ABOUT THE WRITER

Tara started writing fiction when she was in first grade, but she didn't discover the thrill of screenwriting until she studied Communications Media at John Paul the Great Catholic University. Screenplays are her favorite way to tell stories.

Tara resides in Colorado, and in 2016, she became a Consecrated Virgin Living in the World in the Diocese of Colorado Springs. In addition to making things up and writing them down, Tara enjoys praying, hiking (definitely not running), going to the symphony (especially movies at the symphony), discovering new craft brews, and spending time with family and friends.

CPSIA information can be obtained
at www.ICGtesting.com
Printed in the USA
LVHW101058170620
658104LV00013B/482

9 781734 914207